FIC   Nevai, Lucia, 1945-

     Star game

DATE			

Star Game

The Iowa Short Fiction Award

Prize money for the award is provided by

a grant from the Iowa Arts Council

Star Game

LUCIA NEVAI

UNIVERSITY OF IOWA PRESS

IOWA CITY

Fio

University of Iowa Press, Iowa City 52242
Copyright © 1987 by Lucia Nevai
All rights reserved
Printed in the United States of America
First edition, 1987

Book and jacket design by Richard Hendel
Typesetting by G&S Typesetters, Austin, Texas
Printing and binding by Malloy Lithographing, Ann Arbor, Michigan

The publication of this book is supported by a grant from the National Endowment for the Arts in Washington, D.C., a federal agency.

Some of these stories have previously appeared, in slightly altered forms, in the following publications: "Star Game," *Literary Review*; "Mr. Feathers," *Playgirl*; "Diamond Twill," *North Dakota Quarterly*; "Hooked," *Blueline*; "Resident Artist," *Iowa Review*; "The Sad-Womb Son," *Ohio Review*; "Baby Wood" and "'Stranger in Paradise,'" *Iowa Woman*; "Mother's Day," *Prairie Schooner*; "Temp," PEN Syndicated Fiction Project Award, *Newsday Magazine, State Magazine, Chicago Magazine*; "Connor's Lake," *Mademoiselle*, © 1984 by Condé Nast Publications; "Likely Houses," *Great River Review*.

Library of Congress Cataloging-in-Publication Data

Nevai, Lucia, 1945–
Star game.
(Iowa short fiction award)
I. Title.   II. Series.
PS3564.E848S73   1987   813'.54   87-16159
ISBN 0-87745-174-5

For

Philip,

who sounded the timbers

of these stories

Contents

Temp

WELCOME TO INTERNATIONAL PAPER, my assignment form reads. INTERNATIONAL PAPER PERMITS PANTSUITS OR PANTS WITH A BLAZER. SHOULD YOU ARRIVE FOR WORK IN DUNGAREES, YOU WILL BE ASKED TO RETURN TO YOUR AGENCY. REPORT TO: ———————————.
The personnel director writes "Mr. Moehl" in the blank with a ballpoint pen. She has a regressive, insecure personality, according to my handwriting-analysis class. I thank her—I'm in my silk blouse and pearls, my pencil-slim wool skirt. I don't swing my hips on the way out her door. I save that for Mr. Moehl.

The elevators look like giant brushed-chrome refrigerators. Chimes announce each opening of a door; the effect is narcotic. My car fills in an orderly fashion and shoots up forty-two floors before I can figure out who's wearing Joy. The halls are carpeted and fluorescent. Everything's manila, the color of files.

Someone in a pleated plaid good-girl skirt is waiting for me. "Hel-lew," she sings. Her name is Aster. She shows me to my work station, a steel desk next to hers. Mr. Moehl's walnut door is locked. "He's not coming in until ten," she says.

"Fine," I say. So far, so good.

I watch Aster water her plants and pick off the dead leaves. She has forgettable hair and a forgettable face, but her manner is measured, authoritative. She pours a bag of candy, cinnamon balls and peppermints, into a glass jar.

"What's that I hear going clink-clink-clink?" says a tall woman, trotting up to Aster's desk. The woman's makeup is fresh; she wears a scarf over a passive angora sweater.

"Grace, this is the temp," Aster says.

"Pleased to meet you," Grace says to me. They suck on cinnamon balls and complain about someone they refer to only as "she." I look around. International Paper has decorated the walls with four-color nature prints, rushing blue streams, a paranoid fall reeling with orange and red, male and female cardinals perched on separate boughs in a tree. I think of all the birds evicted to make pink While You Were Out pads.

3

"Good morning, Jesus," Aster says in a cutesy-coo voice. A stainless steel mailcart rolls past my desk, propelled by a very handsome Hispanic. He wears a green polyester service coat, as if he needed identification or we needed protection or something. He slips a stack of pink, blue, and yellow envelopes into my in box, another stack into Aster's. She offers him the candy jar. He thinks she wants him to take it somewhere. "No, dummy," she says in the baby voice. "Have one."

The pink, blue, and yellow envelopes contain priority-coded interoffice memos. Pink is urgent, so we open those first; then we open blue and, last, yellow. We throw all the envelopes away. I've never seen such a waste of paper.

From nine to ten Aster sits at her desk reading a contemporary romance, and I sit at my desk writing one. My romance features a spirited and intelligent woman between the ages of eighteen and thirty, like the publisher's guidelines specify. She is beautiful, maybe not to everyone but at least in the eyes of the hero. He should be tall, dark, and handsome, but I'm making him blond. She has personal problems, but they are limited to jealousy and stubbornness. She isn't a virgin, but her sexual encounters with the hero are the best she's had. I'm supposed to use euphemisms, especially when referring to below-the-waist. I don't care if I publish it. I write the way some people chew gum.

Mr. Moehl trips on a wave in the swollen carpet as he bolts past my desk, smiling at me. He's on the heavy side, his face is red, his eyes friendly. Aster's boss is younger and meaner. He wants Aster to get Mr. Moehl on the phone, though their offices are side by side. I watch them talk to each other, their feet up on the desks as they look out their big Park Avenue windows.

Mr. Moehl buzzes me in to take dictation. Dictation makes me feel subversive. I know what I look like in my silk and pearls. My skirt falls open at the knee when I cross my legs. I sit there with licked lips, pencil poised over pad, trying to get a rise out of Mr. Moehl. He dictates the usual "it has come to my attention that" to inferiors, "I am pleased to report that" to superiors. His word "operationalization" looks ridiculous in shorthand. He is a nice slow dictator. Whenever I look up, I seem to catch him in some awkwardness, pulling up a droopy sock, poking something in his eye. Mr. Moehl is beyond rises and he knows I know it. He tries to make friends by showing me his wife and his boat, both framed on his desk. I let him off the hook, give him an extra swing of the hips on my way out his door, which I regret when he calls me back in, coughing apologetically.

He hands me a legal-size table filled with numbers, a sheepish look on his face. He needs the table retyped and fifty copies by two o'clock. "Fine," I say. He makes a few more calls, then bolts out of his office, just missing the wave in the carpet this time, smiling at me gratefully, late for a meeting.

Aster hears the slow tick-tock-tock of my typewriter and knows I'm typing numbers. "Did he give you that inventory table for Cleveland?" she asks. "Don't do it."

"I don't mind," I say.

"Don't do it *yet*," she explains. "He'll change it five minutes after you're done and you'll have to redo the whole thing."

"He's one of those?" I ask.

"He never gets anything right," she says in the cutesy-coo voice. "He's a dodo bird."

"I've got nothing better to do," I say. I'm sick of my romance. Jesus comes down the hall with more mail. He hands Aster the new *Cosmopolitan* and they take a few minutes to thumb through it.

"How to spot a potentially cruel lover," Aster reads aloud.

"This I must know," Jesus says.

"Thirty-six women who were repeatedly attracted to a cruel lover," reads Aster, "said to look for a curiously erect posture that makes him seem remote from all those around him. They said to look for a surprising hostility in the first encounter."

I stop typing numbers. I feel myself turning white. I bend

over to hide my face, pretending to make order of my lower right drawer.

"Ask him about his friends," Aster reads. "He won't have any. Ask him about his childhood. He will never have a warm or funny anecdote to tell. Ask him about his philosophy of life. Dog-eat-dog, he'll say." Aster looks at Jesus thoughtfully. "Poor guy," she says in her baby voice.

"Poor girls," Jesus says. "You don't know these types." Aster's boss comes out of his office with work for her. Jesus moves down the hall behind the mailcart, his sinewy shoulders rippling under the synthetic coat.

"I may be a little late back from lunch," Aster warns me at noon. The pope is in New York today; she wants to try to catch a glimpse of him and his entourage parading down Fifth. She buttons up her coat, pulls on her mittens, winds her scarf around her neck with charming decorum, as if she is going to church.

"Take your time," I say. I get out my container of coffee yogurt and my stainless steel spoon. As soon as Aster's gone, I dial 887-6110 and let it ring. And ring. And ring. My chest is heaving. The tall blond man who isn't home has left little bruises inside my thighs. It was the party of a friend of a friend. His blue eyes were like floodlights. He assumed I recognized him from his TV commercials, but I'd never seen him before. We ended up in the coats, the furs piled on the loft bed. He was a rammer and he swore at me softly while he rammed. I try again. No answer. All day Sunday I waited for him where he told me to wait. Don't these actors have answering services? What if this was an audition call?

I take a message for Aster While She Is Out. When I slip the message in her stork message clip, I notice the miniature kingdom that surrounds her chair—a koala hanging in the philodendron, a butterfly paperweight, an orange rubber cat perched on the Kleenex box. I don't want to be like thirty-six other women who were repeatedly attracted to a cruel lover. I don't want to be like anyone.

TEMP

Mr. Moehl does change the numbers. I'm whiting out and typing in new digits when Aster comes back. She saw the pontiff, I hear her tell Grace. I traipse down the hall to the copy center, push my way through the glass double doors, and stand in line. I feel happily hypnotized by the smooth, precise clicking and feeding noises of the Xerox 7000, pumping out piece after piece of hot paper like some tireless Formica heart. Down goes my original on the glass plate. PRINT, I command, pushing the biggest button, green. I plop the fifty immaculate copies, still warm, on Mr. Moehl's desk and pause—he's still out—to enjoy his view of the skyscraper across Park.

I don't enjoy it. I'm glad I'm only spending one day in this corporation.

The new chart is completely wrong. I sit at my desk from four o'clock on, putting Mr. Moehl through to our office in Cleveland twenty times and twenty times changing the numbers. I resent obeying. I resent typing 769,100,322 in a column only wide enough for 8,433,581. I look at my high heels lying on the manila carpet where I have kicked them. They have lost their sleek manufactured form and have adopted the bumps of both my big toe joints. I don't know whether to loathe them because they show my true shape or respect them because they no longer lie. I think about my college bio lab partner, Galen something. He wrote me interesting letters from the Arctic which I never answered. He treated *me* like the wild one who could be patiently tamed. Usually it's the other way around. Tick-tock-tock. I've reached the zombie stage, making as many wrong entries as correct ones.

Mr. Moehl asks me to call his wife. I surprise myself and Aster, who is listening, by first dialing my happily married old friend Charlie. It's funny—I only meet Charlie four times a year and I never know until I pick up the phone when the next time is going to be. "Hi, it's me," I say, picturing both of us naked on my fake-fur rug. In three seconds I have a date. I feel so much better. I feel like a hell of a lot more than a set of ten fingertips.

"She's not finishing this tonight!" Aster yells into Mr. Moehl's office without getting out of her chair. "She has to come back tomorrow!" At five to five, her desk is clean, her out box empty, her hands folded on her blotter. I fold my hands on mine.

While we are waiting for the elevator, Aster tells me the story of her dachshunds. The first one, Winky, she had eleven years. He got cataracts and had to be put to sleep. She gave him a special cremation. Aster's second dachshund was a girl, Missy, who died too after only three and a half weeks. Viral encephalitis. Her new Missy is doing fine. She follows Aster from room to room—she runs. She forgets to slow down on the kitchen linoleum. She slips and slides and makes Aster laugh. Aster shows me a snapshot of a lampshade. Off center in the greenish dark are two ruby eyeballs. "Cute," I say.

The elevator chimes. "See you tomorrow," we both say in the lobby. Sometime between the revolving door and the subway stairs, between a red light and a green, between my right foot and my left, I begin to need a true and lasting love.

Mother's Day

From age five to twenty, Jorie spent Sunday mornings singing alto in a Methodist choir in the middle of Indiana. It was your basic tonic, dominant, subdominant, tonic. The words, when they made sense, were seldom relevant: "Rock of ages, cleft for me, let me hide myself in Thee."

When Jorie got married and moved to the suburbs of New York City, Sunday mornings became a blank. Nothing took the place of the idle harmony, the simple procedure of standing up with a hymnbook to sing. Her B.A. thesis on Wallace Stevens left her expecting some mature new ritual, as in the opening lines of his poem "Sunday Morning":

> Complacencies of the peignoir or late
> Coffee and oranges in a sunny chair.

Instead she battled despair. When something did emerge, fifteen years later, it was bawdier than the poem and a bit more hurried.

It begins with a jog by the Hudson River with her second husband, Paul, a Brooklyn-born Jew, and ends with their sweat pants in a heap on the Sunday *Times*. His daughters are with their mother; her sons are with their father. The phone inevitably rings and their eyes open, fixing the image of their coupling. His skin is opaque, hers translucent against the blood- and curry-colored patterns of the prayer rug. The answering machine silently swallows the message, its red light flashing.

"'Brawl'!" The voice on the tape is cheerful and triumphant. "A five-letter word for 'Donnybrook' with an A in the middle is 'brawl'!" It's Margaret, Jorie's mother, calling long distance from Indiana. She's just arrived home from the annual Mother's Day buffet at the Sherwood Cafe. Jorie and Paul made their holiday calls early, leaving Margaret with a crossword query from the *Times* puzzle.

The other call is for Paul. It's his daughter Michelle, canceling their date. Jorie is disappointed for him and for herself—she was hoping for a duet from Nick and Jake. A raucous, even irreverent "Happy Mother's Day" would do. They are twelve and ten, too young to think of calling on their own. And since Alex, their father, believes *his* mother is the only real mother, Nick and Jake are probably chanting those three words to her instead.

"Michelle has done that to me the last two times," Paul says, dialing to see if Becky is canceling too. Jorie is impressed that he can make these calls stark naked. "She goes out dancing until four in the morning, then—"

"It's the age," Jorie says. Michelle is sixteen, Becky fourteen. Jorie has not found a way to connect with them yet.

"Let me talk to your sister," Paul says to Michelle, loading on the guilt. Jorie leaves to straighten the living room. "*Where* are we going? We're going to the *zoo*," she hears him say. "Yes, the zoo *again*. No, we're not going shopping first. I hate shopping. Go shopping with Mom." There is a long pause, presumably while he listens to Becky's case. "Nope, sorry," he says. "No one is too old for the zoo. Be ready."

He wants to impress his daughters with his values to counter what he imagines are the values of Howard. Howard is a young fast-track stockbroker who is hanging out with Paul's exwife, Freddie. She is a former actress, still beautiful, charming, vital. A flashy dresser, she has recently and unexpectedly come into money.

Jorie is a small-boned prairie type. "Earthy, with a celestial face," is Paul's description.

"Wait," she says when he is dressed. She stands on tiptoe and fusses with his silk scarf. Jorie is a social worker and he likes her to work on him too, even if it's just his scarf. He gives in with a docile expression to her pale, precise hands, flicking, folding, patting—a visual paradox, for he is a big, burly man, swarthy-skinned and silver-haired.

Jorie never expected to find such a felicitous ally in someone basically so foreign. He runs his sports magazine like a
hood, reserves his philanthropic urges for his family—the opposite of her first husband's orientation.

"There," she says. As Paul unlocks the door, the docile look
is replaced by what Jorie calls his bored look. She loves the
dark, ironic eyes with their lazy lids, the sly, self-deprecating
smile. "Bored again!" she laughs.

"I'm a bored-again Jew."

The stillness of the apartment gives Jorie a moment's panic.
Since her divorce, all stillnesses contain an echo of separation.
In Riverside Park, the widows are beginning to leave the
wooden benches, their old spring coats too thin for the four
o'clock chill.

Ten years ago, Jorie was at the Sherwood Mother's Day buffet too. The day really belonged to Margaret, who was photo-
graphed for the local paper wearing her orchid corsage. At
fifty, she was never more handsome, proud that her daughter
on her right had produced two excellent baby boys, relieved
that *her* mother on her left was not dead.

Jorie had saved the clipping, though to her the snapshot told
too much. Her grandma's eyes were lined with pain, the irises
cloudy, drifting, vague. The mouth was set to endure—unlike
Jorie's. A tense, forced smile was trapped on Jorie's face. She
wasn't ready for the photograph. She had been thinking about
having her first affair.

Now her grandma is dead and her mother is drifting toward
vagueness, though less today than other days.

Jorie has two hours to kill before she will have to roll up
her sleeves to handle the arrival of Nick and Jake. It's curious
the way they take turns being difficult during the custodial
transition. She never knows whose turn it is. There's no explanation, not even a clue. She pencils the word "brawl" into the
puzzle spaces.

Classical music is playing on the radio in Jake's room. The door will open no more than a foot before it jams up against a sea of cardboard boxes and radio parts. There's a robot under construction. Jake needs company—he doesn't like any of the kids in the fifth grade. Jorie peers around the door.

Jake is swinging back and forth in his hammock. He is busy drawing boxes on lavender construction paper. His baseball cap is pulled down almost over his blue eyes. He's handsome in an aloof way that makes people stare. His solution is to hide under hats.

"Jake," Jorie says, "I can't get in."

"That's okay."

"Well, take your juice then." She holds out the glass.

He doesn't look up or budge. "Grape or *apple?*" he asks mistrustfully.

"Grape, for Chrissake."

Jake gets out of the hammock to take the glass.

"Anything happen this weekend?" she asks.

"No."

So it's not Jake, she thinks. She looks around the room at his array of interesting projects—puppets, computers, space villages—and now this robot. Somehow, it collectively makes up for his lack of communication. What he thinks or feels has always been a mystery, even to him.

"Want a good-night kiss?" she asks.

"No, thanks."

Jorie is leaving Jake's room for Nick's when she hears Paul's key in the lock. His silk scarf is now a mess. "The most amazing thing happened," he says, his eyes dancing.

"I have to talk to Nick first," she stops him.

He frowns. "Whenever."

"You spend too much time with Jake," Nick says, folding his arms over his bare chest with a pained, spoiled air. He is sitting up in bed, a crisp new X-MEN comic in his lap. The room is spare, but the rock posters on the walls give it a frenetic, airless quality.

"That's physically impossible," Jorie says, seating herself on the bed and handing him a glass of milk. He studies the surface of the milk and makes a face, then lifts something off with the pad of his finger and wipes it on the bedspread.

"There's always a black dot," he says. "If you look closely at anything you eat, you'll see it."

He puts the glass on his night table, where Jorie will find it in the morning, still full. She strokes his dark curls. He has his father's coloring and temperament.

She has to be careful—adoration and irritation are equal pitfalls.

Nick gets a look in his eyes as if he's about to say something candid. It's time to test Jorie for vestiges of commitment to Alex. She feels suddenly tired.

"Paul tries too hard," Nick says.

"He just *got* here," Jorie points out, but Nick goes on.

"He tries to force us to like him by telling us children's stories." His eyes flare with arrogance.

"That's not so terrible, is it?" Jorie asks. It's a comment she learned from the guidance books. Nick's mouth relaxes into a grin. She waits for the next subject.

"Mom?" His eyes regain their haughty, slighted look.

"What?"

"Daddy sold the red car."

Jorie hardens. She isn't up to red car stories. She wishes she had never taught Nick to like them.

The red car stories started when she needed a way to mold her husband to fit family life. His behavior, at times, was out of control. In Indiana, the family rule was to absolve blunderers by making a funny story out of the inconvenience. It was curious how once Jorie began applying the rule to Alex, it was impossible to stop.

He would drive over the hilly country roads at a hundred miles an hour, late to his mother's, and she would tell the boys it was a roller coaster ride. He would drive backward around the suburban streets to make them laugh, and she made fun of the gawkers. He would drive through the junk at the dump until a coil spring mattress curled up like a jelly roll under the chassis. The red car couldn't go forward or backward. They were stranded for hours—they missed a plane—but she joked about the junk they scavenged for the TV room. In the red car too, Alex would bring home odd, helpless people who needed food and shelter. She gave them code names, winking at the boys, and took it up with Alex privately.

Her generosity was not reciprocated. The red car stories got worse and some could not be told at all.

When she gave up, the boys considered her a fraud. The red car stories memorialized their father's impulsiveness while omitting its cost to her. Now they had to pay.

They both feel honor-bound to snub Paul, who has made their job too easy by craving their companionship.

"He sold it. Somebody bought it," Nick states as if this was inconceivable. Jorie is silent, begrudging him the subject. "They drove it right out of the driveway," he says. There is a minute tremor in his chin.

"Must have been hard for you," Jorie concedes. "Guess I felt that way about my daddy's green Ford."

Nick's brittle nod is almost imperceptible. Now that the pain is shared, it's not so bad.

"Remember the dump," she says softly.

Nick perks up. "Remember driving backward?" he asks. They both laugh.

"Remember the mailbox?" Nick asks. He's proudest of that story, though Jorie tries to forget it. *He* was at the wheel, shifting gears until the red car rolled down the side yard and into the mailbox across the street. Jorie saw him from the kitchen window and he waved, wondering why her face was white. He was three.

"I wanted to *dwive*," he giggles. Jorie is grateful when he regresses, even for a second. When he holds out his arms for a good-night hug, his embrace is energetic. More than I get from Jake, she thinks.

Paul is sitting at the kitchen table in his Brooklyn Dodgers T-shirt, poring over the sports section.

Jorie fills the teakettle with good cold tap water for their tea and sets it on the gas flame. "What was so amazing?" she asks.

He lights a cigarette and leans back on two legs of the chair. "So here's the story. Bitch, bitch, bitch all the way to the zoo. We get there. All she says is 'so what.' The zebra, the giraffe, the penguins—even the *penguins*—get a 'so what.'

"'Look,' I say, 'I need this like a hole in the head.' I head for the gate. There's a big crowd. We hear some guy shouting, 'Hey, you! Whatcha gonna do? Hey, muthuh, lessee whatcha got!' Sounds like a fight. I feel like punching somebody myself, so I push my way through the crowd, and Becky, she follows me.

"Turns out it's not a fight. It's some jerk—a little macho guy in tight pants, shirt unbuttoned to here, gold chains—standing in front of the lion's cage with his buddies, giving the lion a hard time. He's spitting, he's throwing stones, and his buddies are eating it up.

"Now the lion isn't moving. He looks like he's four thousand years old. He's lying down against the bars with his back to the guy. His balls are already busted from being in the cage, and now some asshole is throwing rocks at him and he's got to take it. The rest of us middle-class animal-rights defenders are getting upset, but we're afraid to say anything because this gang looks rough."

As Paul warms to his story, his voice gets louder and louder. Jake wanders into the kitchen. "Too loud," he complains half-heartedly. Beneath his fake annoyance, he is brimming with curiosity. "I can't sleep."

Jorie holds out her arms. He comes to sit in her lap, handing her the lavender construction paper he was working on in his hammock.

"Go ahead," Jorie says to Paul without looking at the paper.

"So the gang is egging this guy on," Paul continues. "And the guy picks up a *stick*. He starts poking the lion in the back with the stick."

Jorie hears a snort. It's Nick, standing in the door in his robe. "What's *he* doing up?" Nick interrupts.

"Shhhh!" Jorie puts a finger to her lips to keep the attention on Paul. Nick snorts again and ensconces himself in the doorway, his face turned away, proving he's there not to hear the story but to keep the bedtime score even.

Paul is encouraged. He jumps out of his chair and struts about as the macho guy, sprawls listlessly on the linoleum as the lion. As he collects the eyes of the boys, Jorie quickens with hope. She sees Jake's lips in profile, slack with absorption. Nick's mouth is tense—he identifies with the lion.

"So the guy is poking the lion in the back with this stick. 'Daddy!' Becky says. 'Do something!' So I decide to stop this guy. I push forward through the gang—" Paul's voice is a bellow now. "But the old lion, he beats me to it. He jumps to his feet, like he's going to walk away, but what he does is lift his leg and piss backward right through the bars onto this guy's chest!"

Jake and Nick erupt in laughter, their eyes connecting with each other, then returning to Paul.

"The gang takes off—they think they're next! And the rest of us cheer."

Jake and Nick clap.

"Becky talked about it all the way home," Paul says to Jorie. "You like that?" he says to the boys, his smile almost maternal. "Wait! Here's an even better one." As Paul launches into another zoo story, Jorie does not move or breathe too deeply, for fear of disturbing the thread-thin roots the men are putting down. She prays that the teakettle, pushing its load of water to a boil, will take a while to sing. Someday, if she has her way, the funny stories told in this room will be about the four of them.

Nick is the first to catch on to her. He pokes Jake, breaking the spell. The story fizzles out in their scuffle. Jorie dismisses them. They try out Paul's lion-pissing gesture on each other as they careen out of the kitchen. Paul returns to the sports section. Jorie slowly unfolds the lavender paper Jake has given her.

To Mom—Love, Jake, it reads across the top. *Do the puzzle and see what it says.* Below is an H-shaped crossword puzzle, the boxes drawn with thick lines. There are only three words. Jorie reads the clues:

> *One—Opposite of Sad.*
> *Two—Opposite of Father's.*
> *Three—Opposite of Night.*

The Nile

Sam stands naked at the tiny wall-hung sink, patting tap water all over her body. She's tall; a thick blond braid hangs down the center of her back. Light from a peach-colored lamp illumines the gentle rhythm of her hands. Her blue eyes are lusterless, her jaw still as stone. The dust of Cairo is everywhere.

Watching her, Len gets aroused. His eyes are excitable, intelligent, insecure; his graying hair is wild at the temples. He loads his Polaroid. He frames her at the sink with one arm missing like the Venus de Milo. He shoots again, a column of light between her thighs. He crouches beneath her and snaps: her pubic hair is blond and straight, the labia coiled beneath, organized as pecan meat. He lines up the Polaroids, exciting himself.

Sam towels herself dry. She waits for Len in their narrow blue bed. The floor tilts—the room is cheap, a tiny double in a houseboat hotel anchored somewhere down the Nile. Sam can't get used to the angle; Len finds it amusing. He lies down and pulls her against him, dizzying her with fondling and stroking. She feels herself falling backward for miles. Sam feels removed from her body, displaced to the side, like the ghost in a double exposure. Len is athletic and vigorous, hammering away enviably at her double. She can't let go. She notices she disguises this by changing positions, once and then again. He tires a little; Sam finds a strand of sensation and rides it to the end. She feels happier.

Len falls asleep easily; his hot, sunburned arms and legs soak Sam with sweat where they touch. Her neck and shoulders are as stiff as cement. She closes her eyes and waits to see if she will drop off. The Nile rolls beneath her like a beast turning over. She is afraid of it. She thought it would be emerald green, romantic, renewing. It is not. It is sluggish and dull, unpredictable. She dreamed she fell into it; she had to lie there for four thousand years before being discovered. Her skull was gone—all that was left was a white rib cage, awake and unsettled in the sand beneath the Nile, a pair of nervous skeletal hands still trying to cover something up.

Sam sleeps well at home in Wilmette. She never has nightmares. She and Len get along well. They go places arm in arm. People think he worships her. It was the Nile that woke her that first night, the Nile rolling over. It was the nightmare.

Tonight she is afraid she will dream about the King's Chamber, a black granite tomb in the center of the Great Pyramid. With two other couples, she and Len crawled through a long dirt-walled tunnel. Sam was afraid she would be crushed; she almost turned back. Though the tomb itself was spacious and the black walls solid, she felt sure that any minute everything would collapse. She stood there, rigid, wary, as the Egyptian guide patted the king's black sarcophagus with a familiar domestic gesture. Though the lid was closed, he explained in terrible English, the spirit of the king could escape at night to visit the spirit of the queen. A British bride in starched bermudas laughed at his explanations, his English; her laugh, a cockney waterfall stopped short with a snort, echoed against the granite walls. Sam thought it was all very frightening and morbid; Len thought it was spiritual.

Len sees majesty everywhere in Egypt—in the exploited ruins, the walleyed cripples. Sam has to hold the white-framed images of his Polaroids in her palm to appreciate what they've seen. What she's seen instead of the sights is that she's afraid of Len; she's not afraid of him at home. It must be nerves, lack of sleep. For five nights they've been in Cairo, and she has stood up through most of them.

Sam wraps herself in a white cotton robe and stands in the dark on the balcony. She listens to the drinkers in the bar across the pier. The drinkers speak Greek; they are men, of course. Sam envies men their freedom to go into any bar in the world and order a drink at any hour. She is sick of the Cairenes—the visible Cairenes are mainly men, men with black eyes instantly assessing the degree of her gullibility, stealing views of her yellow hair from Len like it was money. The air is thick over the Nile, smearing the glow of three lights on the other side. Sam feels corrupt, a feeling that comes, she assumes, with fatigue. She holds herself in her arms and waits for dawn.

Len has been all over on grants and fellowships—to Peru, to Turkey and Greece, to Mexico, Israel, Morocco, but never to Egypt, never with Sam. Their itinerary, Cairo, Luxor, Aswan, is his gift to her on their anniversary. They will follow the Nile, deeper and deeper into the desert, their treat for getting through ten years of marriage. His Polaroids will form a new folio; Len is a professor of photography at a fine arts institute in Chicago. People who know his work know Sam by heart too, though not the intimate details. Just the face, the hair, the throat, the long beautiful back. When people meet her, they are surprised that her mood is different from the mood in the photographs. Sometimes they are disappointed; sometimes they are intrigued. Sam has stopped caring who is what. She used to paint. She never has shows anymore—she hasn't taught art in years—but Len continues to introduce her as a painter. Sam loves Len, though she left him once. She came back and now it's ten years.

Luxor is hotter than Cairo. It is quieter. The natives move more slowly. They are more hopeless. Len wants to find a room to let. The taxi driver takes them to his mother's house, a strip of rooms in a narrow alley with a shared, rudimentary bath. Sam says no. She wants a first-class hotel. "A good bed, a good bath," she says to Len. "Otherwise I won't be able to sleep."

"How am I supposed to pay for it?" he asks.

"Charge it." She shrugs, exasperating him. Both their faces are rigid as the taxi drives them to the Winter Palace. They interrupt the silence to accuse each other briefly.

"Don't you know what the tickets are costing?"

"I thought this was something to celebrate. How many of our friends are still together?"

The Winter Palace is on the Nile. The Nile is narrower here

and brown. Sam loves their room—it's high, beautifully shuttered, white. The bathroom tile is a frantic blue. For her, the argument is over. She unpacks with energy and conviction.

"Isn't it worth it?" she cries. She notices her voice is shrill. Len is changing his shirt. Sam wants to stop him but she doesn't know how. She tries embracing him, making him look at her face, the face he is weak for, the face that fills his negative files. "Take a bath with me?"

He won't answer. He won't look at her.

Water thunders into the huge white porcelain tub as Sam stands in the bathroom doorway watching Len. He is shaving for happy hour. His expression in the mirror is self-absorbed and confident. Each stroke of the razor excites anxiety in Sam.

The waiter's hand extends from the starched, embroidered cuff of his jellaba like a gnarled brown root. He feigns a continental flick of the wrist as he lifts some kind of meat from the platter onto Sam's plate. Len is already tasting his. He was served first. Sally and Gail were served next. Sally and Gail are two girls from California whom Len has befriended at the bar. Sally has bushy dark hair. Both her eyeteeth protrude, giving her smile an innocuous, civic quality. Gail is a brunette, fresh-looking and freckled, a little masculine about the throat and shoulders. Sam slices her meat in two, then rests her knife and fork on the plate parallel to each other.

"Mmmmm!" Sally shrieks, pointing at Len's belt buckle. She finishes chewing, then strokes the molded brass. "Where'd you get this?"

"San Francisco."

"I knew a guy who made belt buckles in San Francisco, but they weren't this big." Sally taps the buckle again and turns to Gail. "Remember Carl?"

"When did you get it?" Gail asks. "Was it recently?"

Sam watches the muscle in Len's jaw flex as he chews. He

wipes his lips with the Winter Palace linen; she is aware of the smell of his after shave.

"No," he says. "It was a long time ago. Before I met Sam." He plants his eyes on her, challenging her to join in. She will not. She joined in once—but never again.

"Len says you paint," Gail says, turning suddenly to Sam. Sam wonders how to answer; she decides to tell the truth.

"I don't," she says. "Not anymore."

"Is that true?" Gail asks Len. Len and Sally break their gaze so Len can answer.

"Is what true?"

"That she doesn't paint anymore, or is she just being modest?"

"She paints," Len insists. "You did that series."

Sam draws a blank. For five years, her brushes have stood clean and dry in a rubber-banded bouquet in a vase. "The red series," Len coaches.

"Oh, that." An embarrassed look flickers over Sam's face and she lowers her eyes. "That wasn't painting. That was more like . . . wallowing. I used a palette knife. That was years ago. I never showed those awful things to anyone." She raises her eyes. No one is listening. She pushes her chair back from the table and stands up behind it.

"Full?" Len asks.

"Yes." The food is still on her plate. She extends her hand to Sally. "Nice to meet you," she says. Sally's hand is cold and dry. "Gail." Gail's hand is rougher and sweatier.

Sam is lying awake in the dark of the room when Len enters sometime after two. She hears him flip on the bathroom light. His belted pants drop with a clink to the floor. She listens while he brushes his teeth. She knows each moment where the brush is in his mouth, which teeth are getting the attention they need. He slides into bed with his back to her. He smells like flowers. Sam envies the familiar phrasing of his breath as he drops off to sleep. Her throat is painfully dry. The pressure on her neck and shoulders is sharp and final. She sits up in bed, her back against the wall, her jaw rigid.

The balcony is a low clay pen the color of tan makeup. Sam sits there for hours the next day, her shoulders hunched against the wicker chair. Her jaw remains rigid. Her eyes are on the Nile. She is starting to hate that word, that single, deceptively smooth syllable. Her blue eyes grow bright with pain.

Len is an hour away in the desert, descending three hundred steps to a maze of tombs. Kings are buried there, more kings, dozens of kings, sixty. Sam planned to go. She made it as far as the lobby, then backed out; she needed time alone to hate, to heal. They both knew this. But Sam can't hate or heal like she does at home. The light of Egypt is too strong, exposing her. She can't change Len—she's tried and failed. She can't leave him—she's tried and failed. People want her to try again, but people don't know everything. She is not capable. There's a reason, but reasons don't matter.

She accepts the weight of her situation, which bears down on her shoulders like thousands of tons of stone. The weight is love—not real love, but the habit they have of calling what they say and do love. A cockney laugh echoes inside her. She wants to rebel, to let it all fall, but she's afraid she'll be crushed. Holding it up, letting it fall—either way she gets crushed. She laughs a short, bitter blast. She hears the weary scratching of rakes below as the natives sweep the Winter Palace walks. She feels lighter. Her jaw relaxes. The love is going, going, gone. Happy Anniversary.

Her hair bleached, her face a dark rose, Sam is still on the balcony when Len returns. "Hey," he says.

"Hey."

"Guess who they know?"

"Who *who* knows?" Why should Len think she knows everything he's thinking?
"Sally and Gail," he says.
"Who do they know?"
"Ray Silberman." He yawns. A donkey tethered somewhere
below brays.
"Ray Silberman," she says. "No kidding."
Len lingers on the balcony, waiting for her to prosecute him.
She usually prosecutes; he usually denies; she weeps; he rapes
her. They've worked it out; it takes an hour and a half; they
emerge arm in arm, happily married. Len's smile grows sheepish now, his eyes apprehensive as Sam remains still, her jaw
slack. He drifts out of her sight. She looks at his Polaroids. The
image that hurts is not one of another woman; it is a pharaoh
and his queen. The pharaoh towers above a colonnade of lime-
stone pillars; the pillars look soft as skin; they are bulbous
on top like erections. The pharaoh's face is half-eroded; his
queen, trapped between his legs, comes up only to his knees.

The handsome Old Cataract Hotel is sprawled, like everything else in Egypt, on the Nile; the river is dark and shallow,
almost at a standstill. The verandah railings are painted a
glossy asian red; the awnings are british green; the canvas
cushions are a saturated, faithful turmeric yellow. Sam can almost feel the pigments—the colors are so visceral she wants
to paint.
She climbs the massive grand staircase with its faded Oriental runner to change into her bathing suit. She has come
back early from the bazaar to swim. Aswan is the hottest place
she has ever been. She hangs her souvenir—a brass hand with
eyes in every fingertip—on their four-poster bed.
The black pool steward watches Sam mount the diving
board and walk to the end. Joylessly, he takes in what he can
of her nakedness, sneaking it from Len who is on his way to
the Aswan Dam, maybe the Unfinished Colossus too, depend-

ing on how hot it gets. Sam loves the rattly rebound of the board, the brief airborne launch, the cold, condensed sensation of her forehead entering a new element. The pool steward watches her stroke to the end of the pool, turn underwater, and stroke back ten, fifteen, twenty times. No one really swims at the Cataract.

Two Frenchwomen stand in the shallow end, splashing their throats and arms as if the water was cologne. Sam climbs out and unravels her braid to dry. "Oooooooh!" the Frenchwomen say, admiring the waist-length hair that falls around Sam like a wavy tent. She stretches out in the sun, closing her eyes. She is so pleased with everything that she is taken by surprise when she feels a sudden pang of deep sorrow. Once, a long, long time ago, before she was married, she taught art to children. She loved children and they loved her. The voice of a Muslim muezzin, calling people to afternoon prayers, rises from a mosque on the hill north of Aswan. His voice is beautiful and earnest. Tears roll down Sam's cheeks.

A shadow darkens the deep brightness filling her closed lids. The pool steward is standing over her, looking down. "Telephone, missus," he says with the elegant African cadence. "Your husband. He is not well."

The depot in downtown Aswan is full, too full. There are twice too many passengers for flight 211. The clerk, a small man with a dishonest face, half-English and half-Egyptian, is under great stress. Everyone wants to go to Cairo. Members of the Egyptian military have business there; the locals have relatives. A planeful of Germans who planned to fly to Abu Simbel today cannot—a sandstorm has obscured the runway; all flights are canceled—but they can't stay in Aswan; there are no rooms. The Germans want to be awarded seats on flight 211 reserved by the Americans, but the Americans don't want to give them up. The Americans want to go home.

Sam is perched on the edge of the divan, on the edge of

everything, waiting for her name to be called. She grasps her ticket, Cairo–Paris–New York–Chicago. Chicago: even the sound of it has a new sense of promise—it sounds quaint, nostalgic, full of color; it sounds like a place where Sam might pick up a paintbrush or teach. It used to sound like a sentence, a cell.

A blue bus is idling outside the depot, waiting to transport the Cairo passengers to the tiny airport ten miles away in the desert. A slow green fan revolves overhead. Len is beside Sam on the divan. He looks like he's flying apart inside; his forehead is white; the gray hair at his temples is tame and damp. Sam checks him for fever; the sting of his skin hurts her because she feels it without loving him, yet the hurt is a victory. All night she was up with him. Every hour she was tempted to give in to the nursing of him and call it love. One slip—one moment of calling it love—and she might have fallen asleep for another ten years. She tried to believe in nothing, but she wasn't strong enough. Casting her eyes around the high, lovely Cataract room at three in the morning, she seized on the lucky brass hand full of eyes from the Aswan bazaar, dangling from the four-poster, winking and waving in the slow night wind. Luck! She believes in luck—lucky 211 to Cairo. One more night in Aswan, one more night nursing Len, and Sam will lose her edge.

The clerk announces a slight delay in the formation of the passenger list. Len drifts to the men's room. Sam defends his seat from the Germans. She opens a copy of the Cairo newspaper to distract herself. Her eyes jump from story to story, picking up morbid pieces. In Jakarta, the bloody scarf of an old woman was found beside tiger footprints; fifty men from her village have set out into the jungle armed with spears and machetes. In Paris, police have recovered a slice of a kidnapped millionaire's finger, wrapped in cotton wool and planted in a railway baggage locker. In England, an anonymous letter has exposed a schoolgirl sex ring catering to "old men, very old men." In Scotland, bloody limbs are being recovered from ditches and streams and car trunks hundreds of miles apart; they appear to belong to a brother and sister. In Russia, milkmaids are drinking themselves to death because there is no place to dance. The only good news comes from Argentina: two Americans are the first to sail over the Andes in a hot air balloon. Up, up, and away! Sam thinks. It might have been luck that got them over!

The clerk clears his throat. He reads the few names he can pronounce—Smith, Johnson. He orders a few members of the army to board the bus. They look frightening to Sam—their eyes are too dreamy; their shirttails are out; their boots are either too large or so small they can't be laced. A rich German and his family of eight are next, a case of bribery, Sam thinks. She watches and waits, perched on the edge of the divan. Each time an American couple is called, they put on their straw hats and push their plaid luggage outside to the bus. Sam misses the plaid and straw; the depot seems more and more foreign without it. The clerk stares at her. He appears to want her yellow braid. She feels like cutting it off and tossing it to him. She rises as he invites "Mr. and Mrs. Sam . . ." to board the blue bus. She hoists the camera bag to her right shoulder, the carryons to her left, and walks outside into the welcome Egyptian light.

The driver waits for Len, who is the last to board. His face is in pieces. The muffler backfires like machine gun fire. The blue bus lurches out of Aswan at ten miles an hour, so slow that the lake of dust rising from the road has time to sift through the windows and settle on the passengers, a fine new layer every mile. The hum of the motor seems to pacify everyone; a stupor envelopes them. Some doze. Sam is so tired she forgets where they are going or how long they have been going there. It comes up suddenly, like a mirage: the tiny terminal, the runway, a truncated strip of asphalt interrupting the desert, the DC-10 shimmering with heat. In the powerful light, everything is all one gold.

Connor's Lake

Connor rides the bulldozer like a motorcycle, hatless in the March cold, his eyes wild above his neat brown mustache. Cursing and reprimanding the earth, he charges up the retaining wall on the dozer and backs down to the right, packing the dirt down, packing it down. Digging his own lake is making a madman out of him. No one in town will ask him how it's going anymore. They're sick of hearing about it. The word is out not to give him excavating jobs—he'll get aggressive and start talking you out of what you want to do.

Meanwhile for him it's no picnic, freezing his butt off every day from dawn to dark, digging a mudhole nine feet deep and an acre wide where his beautiful field used to be. A lot rides on this lake, the least of it being a hundred dollar bet with the agronomist from Albany who told him he'd never get water to stick in that field. "Kroydek or Kroychek, whatever the fuck your name is," Connor shouts into the wind, "there's clay, goddamn it!" He sincerely hopes there is.

Connor works until the dirt and the sky are the same color of purple; then he climbs down off the D-6 and walks up the hill to his cabin. It's hard for him to take any pleasure in his shower. The hot water comes in one stingy, erratic stream—he has to hold himself beneath it ingeniously so that most of the water breaks into a thin wall which warms his broad young back. A shift in weight diverts a trickle to the front to catch his chest. The mud runs off him and down the drain, but there's never really enough hot water to let him forget the two things he's afraid of most: digging a lake that won't hold water and Kaitlin with the long pointed breasts in the health food store who keeps giving him two pounds of dried pineapple rings for the price of one. He feels wary. Connor has never lived through such a prolonged period of being absolutely uncertain that he is doing the right thing. When he steps out of the shower, the towel he grabs is musty and soiled. He pities himself.

Connor sits in his green DeSoto in the Newmans' driveway

for ten minutes before getting out, looking at the glass wall
Richard put in the north side of the barn. It was a year in the
making, the glass wall. Now the Newmans have the best barn
in the woods. The design is impressive, trapezoids of glass
angled artfully in the diagonal cedar siding. Richard designed
it, but the installation was too much for him. He had to hire
people to finish it last November so he and Lilly wouldn't
freeze to death. It cost a fortune.

Connor is jealous of Richard's trust fund. Everyone is. Everyone who's left, that is. Of the ten couples who bought properties in the Minnisink woods in the early seventies, only four
and a half are left. Connor counts himself the half. He and Gita
were the first to discover that farmhouses and barns on several
acres could be had cheap in Minnisink. But now he's alone.
He's been alone since January. He thought it would be much
easier than it is. The truth is, he doesn't know what to do with
himself. He couldn't get through the week without Richard
and Lilly.

The Tiffany lamp over the round oak pedestal table is turned
on. Connor watches Lilly's long beautiful hair fall forward, soft
as corn silk, as she leans across the table to line up a knife and
fork in front of one of the chairs. He watches as she moves
patiently back and forth from the counter to the table with
wine and glasses, two big pottery plates, bowls of salad, and a
basket of something. Of course, Richard doesn't deserve her.
His car isn't even in the driveway. If Connor had a wife like
that, he'd be home for dinner every night.

Connor wipes his mouth with a napkin which he takes a
good look at for the first time. To his consternation it is made
of stiff, batiked cotton. "Jesus Christ," he sneers playfully, tossing the napkin onto the table, "does everything in this house
have to be a *craft?*"

"*I* made those, Connor." Lilly takes him seriously.

He looks at her. She seems a little distracted, but her high white brow is clear of the telltale Richard-trouble furrows. "Where's Richard?" he asks.

"In the city. Realizations."

"I thought he finished that seminar."

"He started the second level of classes. Tuesdays and Thursdays. He leaves at four and he's back at two."

"I hate that shit," Connor scoffs. "Fortunately, he doesn't try to talk me into it anymore."

"It's good for him," Lilly insists. "It keeps him from being depressed, keeps him working."

"That's all fine and good," Connor says, pushing back his chair. "But he acts like a person is betraying him unless they do everything *he* does. I mean, I have realizations of my own. And one of my realizations is that his realizations are horseshit."

Lilly smiles and Connor basks in the approval of her twinkling blue eyes. "It's about time." He grins, referring to her smile. She yawns a large comfortable yawn and stretches her arms up over her head, arching her back. Connor is tempted to ogle the outline of her pretty breasts in the blue turtleneck, but instead he stands up and pulls his jeans out of his crotch. He reaches across the table for Lilly's plate and stacks it on his own so all her gravy slides up under his rim. He takes her buttery knife and neatly licked spoon and lays them side by side with his own sloppy utensils. He sets her wineglass and his on top of the plates with the silver between the stems of both glasses and carries the whole tidy mess to the sink.

He washes everything off methodically with hot running water and some new Swedish natural bristle brush Lilly has come up with. She sits at the table, inert, pressing the tip of her middle finger into the stray salt crystals which catch the light on the unwiped table. He sees her vitamins by the faucet and remembers she's pregnant. He decides he'll take her out to dinner tomorrow so she won't have to cook. Richard too, if he's home. "Why don't you go lie down?" he says proprietarily.

"That's what I'll do," she says, rising and pulling the chain on the Tiffany lamp. Scowling in the dark of the kitchen, Connor scrubs every last bit of Beef Bourguignonne off the black dutch oven and wipes it carefully round and round inside with Lilly's soft white towel.

She's sleeping on the sofa when he comes in to talk. Connor unfolds the afghan and tries to arrange it over her, but it won't reach—her ankles stick out. He positions a fragrant quarter log on the grate and builds the wood around it so the fire will last a long time. Then he lies back on the Oriental rug with a hard little needlepoint pillow under his head. He wonders if Kaitlin flirts with all the health food customers or just him. She's young and almost pretty. She's not intense or high-strung. He's read all her T-shirts. He's measured those long legs against his. He's never had a young, long-legged girlfriend who could give him all the pineapple he wanted.

Round and round, someone is rubbing Connor's shoulder. He climbs slowly out of his dream of being in the post office, screaming at someone who is fucking up his mail. He opens his eyes. Lilly is leaning over him.

"Connor," she whispers, "time to go home."

"What happened?" he asks.

"Nothing. It's late."

"Did we make love?" he jokes. She looks tense and impatient.

"Time to go," she insists. The furrows are there, loud and clear on her white forehead.

"What time is it?" Connor says soberly.

She hesitates and then answers, "Four-thirty."

"Oh, shit. Poor angel," Connor whispers. Richard is seeing the girl from Realizations again. Connor rises slowly to his elbows and then pulls himself into a seated position, gathering Lilly into his arms. She lets him hold her. "Sure you want me to go?" he asks. "I could stay and give you a nice back rub or we could go back to sleep and then go out to breakfast together."

Lilly stiffens slightly and pulls away just enough so that the polite thing for Connor to do is release her. He lets his arms fall to the Oriental rug. He is disappointed. Lilly is too goddamn proud. She wants Connor's car out of the driveway before Richard or anybody else sees it. Appearances first—even though they're all best friends.

All the way back to his house in the dark, Connor can't help wanting Lilly's little game to be tricked up. He can't help wanting Richard to come home early one of these nights and find Connor and Lilly singing "Wake up Little Susie" in perfect Everleys harmony by the fire. Or eating a whole strawberry-rhubarb pie right after they baked it. Or standing outside by the spruce tree listening to the mockingbird.

He wishes Richard would come sailing over the hill at sixty miles an hour right now. He'd like to see the expression change on his dissipated, selfish face as Connor's DeSoto passes him coming from the glass-walled barn. Let Richard be jealous for a change. It would be good for him. Connor thinks this all the way back along Route 38, but Richard's blue Volvo does not come into view at any point.

He parks by the road and sits in the car. He needs to be held. He needs to be hard. Instead of walking into the house and falling asleep in his stale gray-sheeted bed, he wanders down the hill. In the violent, bloody mess of the spring dawn, he kneels in the mud at the edge of the gaping acre-wide hole. It lies there in terrible judgment of him. He remembers what it looked like as a field, its golden silk knee-high with red sumac and white milkweed. He remembers the way the grass would part when anyone walked through it.

Panic rises in Connor's blood and he feels overwhelmed with loss. He sees Gita wading through the field, so skinny and so intense in her long cotton skirts and baggy sweaters. He used to ridicule her for going into the woods with her homeopathic pamphlet listing the Bach Flower Remedies. He wonders why once they were married, he began to despise everything that made her happy. He hopes this is not the closest thing to love that he will ever feel. He's baffled as he remembers the day in January when he found the torn-out page with the list of infusions for despondency. *For despondency through lack of confidence: larch. Despondency through self-reproach: pine. Despondency through anguish: sweet chestnut. Despondency due to embitterment: willow.*

The red slowly drains from the sky. All that's left by six is a pink cast on the stubbly bleached winter grass of the hill. The lake bed is mottled with saturated-looking stretches of gray. "Clay," Connor announces. He leaps to his feet and punches the air with his right fist. "Kroychek, you bastard!" he howls. "Get out your checkbook! There's fucking clay!" He jumps up and down in the mud, hugging himself. By fall, the lake will be filled. By spring, the mud will have settled and the water will be clear. By summer, the lake will be alive with salamanders, leeches, fish eggs, and cattails. Forget-me-nots will bloom on the banks. Turtles will sun themselves on the rocks. All that life will have come from the water.

Connor runs up the hill to shower and shave. He won't work on the lake today. The clay is there—he can relax, finish the hole on weekends. He wants to get back into the swing of things, go into town, hustle up some basements, get a landscaping contract. But first he'll celebrate. He'll buy himself a big breakfast at the Sunrise Diner, read the paper, smoke a cigar, and then, at ten to ten, when Kaitlin pulls into the parking lot of the health food store in her Jeep, sleepy and sexy, fumbling for the key, Connor will be at the door, ready and waiting with a great big order for dried pineapple.

Star Game

For three days the weatherman has promised rain, but rain will not come. The evening air is heavy with suspended moisture. The sun is setting in a colorless haze over Connor's half-filled lake. The picnic he planned to introduce his new nineteen-year-old girlfriend to Lilly and Richard is now a dinner party. It seems all wrong to Lilly to be served Chicken Kiev indoors on Memorial Day, but the Chicken Kiev is ready. It's in the oven on low, adding to the heat.

Lilly feels tongue-tied, watching Connor stretch out against the stone fireplace in his white jeans. He's never looked so relaxed. The desperation is gone from his wonderful craggy face. Now Lilly has it. At six months, she is all spheres. Her pristine Nordic features have fattened into a moon face. Her limbs are waterlogged. Her breasts are brimming out of her peasant dress. She slides her wedding ring up and down the top two joints of her swollen ring finger while Connor describes his garden to her row by row.

"Peas along the fence," he says with a level, patient stroke of the air. "We put the damn peas in three days ago to catch the rain. Corn—same place as last year. The coons leave it alone. Cukes and zukes—next to the corn."

Kaitlin, whom Connor met behind the cash register at the Minnisink Health Food Store, is crouched on enviably lean legs, thumbing through his record collection, hoping to recognize something for dinner music. She has just moved into Connor's cabin, bringing along a few incongruous appliances and furnishings like the plaid wing chair in which Lilly cannot make herself comfortable. Richard is helping to reduce the awkwardness of this first meeting by staying in the bedroom. He's on the telephone long distance to New York with someone from his Realizations group.

"No eggplant this year. And *no* cantaloupe," Connor concludes.

Dangling from the towel bar in Connor's bathroom is a burgundy lace demicup bra, which Lilly now pictures decorating a Burpee seed packet. Connor's eyes, dark and peaceful over his trim mustache, graze the field of air between them. Lilly wants to collect his eyes and focus them on her, where they were all winter, shot through with grief, spilling with desire. With Richard in New York much of the time, it was up to Lilly to get Connor through his divorce. Now, with no token from him of how close they've been, she is ashamed to remind herself of the nights—there were two—when he tried to seduce her.

"Know what?" He smiles.

"What?" She feels puppyish, hopeful.

"I've planted cantaloupe for seven years and I've never had one ripen before frost that didn't taste like shit."

Lilly feels water rising in her eyes. She fusses with the wing chair cushions in order to hide her face. The timer, another Kaitlin import, goes off in the kitchen.

"The rice," Kaitlin says.

"I'll do it," Connor offers, his eyes sliding over her in a routine exercise of possession.

"Thanks, honey." Kaitlin's voice is immensely happy, immensely inexperienced. She turns to Lilly, asking, "Who's Bob Die-lun?"

Lilly sees her then as Connor must: her confidence, her lack of history make her beautiful.

"*Dyl*-an," she coaches gently. "He's one of the songwriters who started the whole folk song thing." She hears condescension creep into her voice. "You probably heard his songs first in the supermarket."

"Oh." Kaitlin has missed the nuances.

Lilly organizes herself to get out of the chair. "Rich-ard!" she calls in her dinner voice as she hoists herself up.

Four footballs of breaded chicken are perched on a bed of cooling rice in the middle of the table. Kaitlin puts the needle on the record she has chosen. As the first charging strains of one of Bach's *Brandenburg* Concertos fill the room, Lilly freezes. Connor rushes over to change the record—his ex-wife's depression lifter, which she would play over and over instead of answering the telephone.

"Is something wrong?" Kaitlin asks.

"Light the candles," Connor says.

Richard bursts from the bedroom as if the evening is only now about to begin. His presence is manic, elegant. He seats Lilly with gallantry. His fine, aristocratic features seem mobilized with an excess of purpose as he lifts his wineglass. "To the four of us," he toasts. "May our love for each other grow and grow." Kaitlin lifts her glass. Lilly is waiting for Connor. Vertical lines form between his eyebrows.

"What's that supposed to mean?" he asks. He wants to fend off any of Richard's double entendres from the start.

"To you and your lady"—Richard makes a point of being insulted—"from me and my lady." The four glasses meet over the platter and clink.

"You people have a very limited idea of love," Richard says, helping Lilly first.

"No lectures," Connor says.

"I'll give you a good example," Richard continues. "Les, the guy I was just talking to, is getting a divorce. It's the most friendly divorce anyone has ever seen."

Lilly pierces her little football of chicken. There is no golden arc of melted butter to prove the dish has been constructed properly. Tasting it, she feels mildly repelled: it's too rich, in a coarse way. Still, she is touched by the image of Kaitlin innocently opening the *New York Times* cookbook to Chicken Kiev. She plays with the vegetables on her plate and eats some of her rice.

"Now Les and Virginia—his ex—talk all the time. They were never able to talk before," Richard says between bites. His table manners are princely. "They even had a good-bye fuck!"

"Pass the rice," Connor barks.

"The good-bye fuck was so good, they had another one!"

Now they're sneaking out on their new relationships to see each other. Les is into creating love for himself. He realizes that just because he's divorcing Virginia it doesn't mean they can't love each other. Love is unlimited. You can have as much love as you want, and then you can have more than *that*, and even more than *that*, and you'll survive!" Richard snickers.

Lilly sees Kaitlin is disturbed by Richard's message of love. She wonders if he has seen the towel bar in the bathroom yet. Connor's head is practically in his plate.

"It's all in your mind," Richard concludes for Kaitlin, tapping his temple twice.

"It's all in your mind," Connor says slowly and firmly.

The night is getting hotter, not cooler. Lilly removes her wedding ring. She and Richard expected a lot out of married life when they commissioned the jeweler to put so much gold in their rings. There is a lull during dessert. Kaitlin drains her brandy blindly.

Lilly retreats into her private custodial relationship with the child inside her. She wants it to be a boy. She wants him to adore her. She wants him to share everything he feels with her. She wants him to succeed. She wants to tell him, very clearly, everything she knows, so he will know it without having to learn it himself. She wants so much for him that she can feel herself toppling into error, but she doesn't know how to step back and want just enough to insure his happiness.

"Who wants to see the lake?" Connor's invitation is greeted with silence all around. Kaitlin stands up to clear the table. A look of urgency invades Richard's features. He excuses himself; soon his voice can be heard on the bedroom telephone, thanking Virginia for what she has done for Les.

"Newman?" Connor only calls Lilly by her last name when he feels like her best friend.

Lilly lets her maternal pondering dissolve. She knows Connor's lake is important to him. He abandoned his excavating business all spring to dig it. Lilly hasn't been down to see it since the week in March when he hit clay. It looked to her then like an acre-wide grave, about the right size to bury his grief in.

"Okay," she says.

"Leave those here."

She kicks off her low-heeled sandals. Connor flips on the porch lamp and lets the screen door slam. The night is starless, the air close. The dry stubble of the grass pokes harshly against the tender skin of Lilly's soles. She inches her way down the hill behind Connor, blinded by the darkness. As they stand level on the dry mud at last, there is no discernible form to the black void that stretches before them.

"Shit," Connor apologizes. "This is the shallow end. She runs north to the aspens and east to the path by the stone wall." Lilly can feel his arm pushing the air past her as he describes the lake with the same strong, level gestures he used on the garden. "She's half-full. The water seeps in from the spring and mixes with the mud bottom. It takes a season or two for the mud to settle."

Lilly hears the soft glup-glup of thick water rocking a wooden boat. "Let's go for a row," Connor says. "Step over here." There is a rustling and the solid knock of wood against wood—the boat against the posts that will someday brace a dock. Connor is cursing softly.

"What's that wonderful smell?" Lilly asks, inhaling the vapors of a pungent, smoky tar that she associates irrationally with the South.

"Creosote," he says. "You always ask me that. Whenever I have the creosote out, you say, 'What's that wonderful smell?'" His disembodied white jeans are floating before her. "Lift your right foot high and step forward," he says. "I'll catch you. Ready?"

"Yes."

"Step."

She follows his directions. Connor grasps her ribs as she

steps forward. Her belly brushes against his chest as he steadies her descent to the soft, wet wood. The boat rocks sluggishly and she finds her balance by sitting on the bench.

"Anchors away," he says, rowing away from the shore. She hears the silky paddle of the oars stroking the water, sees the white jeans on the bench across from her. "Where are we now?" she asks after a while.

"Somewhere near the middle. How do you like it so far?" he laughs, hauling up the oars. In their trajectory, the oars sprinkle cold water on Lilly's arms and thighs. She feels Connor arranging his feet beside her on the bench, imagines him sprawling back against the stern. "Some nights the sky goes on forever," he says. "Tonight it starts and ends right here."

Lilly looks up out of habit. The black haze presses down on her face. She hugs herself—an unpleasant chill rides over her shoulders in the heat.

"You're quiet tonight," Connor says.

"I miss you."

There is a long pause. When his voice comes, it is low and final, the conclusion of an interior debate. "I miss you too."

A bittersweet warmth spreads through Lilly's chest. It's pain: resignation mixing with generosity. "She's nice."

"She's sound. I've never had that before."

There is another long silence. "Well," Lilly says, "we'll have to find a place for her in the star game." Over the years, by assigning them constellations, she and Connor have whimsically chronicled the fortunes of the band of city couples who were the first to own Minnisink County properties. They would sit on Connor's hill, sipping tequila and tracking the progress of their friends in the sky: matches, mismatches, switches, escapes, competitions, punishments. They were clever and arcane.

"Naaaaaah," Connor grunts. He fumbles with his shirt buttons.

So that's over too, Lilly thinks. She sees the white jeans stand upright, hears the zipper unzip. "You're not!" she says.

"I am."

"Is it deep enough?"

The flat crack of Connor's shallow dive is her answer. She and the luminescent white heap of jeans rise and fall in the wake of his lunge from the boat.

"Shiiiiiiiit!" he howls the way he always howls when the water's too cold. Lilly usually matches him skinny-dip for skinny-dip, but this one she happily sits out. She listens to his even strokes in the water, getting farther away from the boat, then nearer. The strokes stop and she hears Connor wading.

"Where are you?" she asks.

"Where am I?" he echoes, using his spooky voice.

Lilly twists on the bench but still can see nothing. She raises her arms protectively, as if she expects him to put a newt down her dress. "Don't scare me, Connor," she orders firmly. The wading stops.

Lightning flashes. For one brilliant instant the setting is flood-lit. Nothing is the way Lilly imagined it. The lake is huge, the banks harsh and devoid of grass. The water is black as pitch, the aspen grove ominously white. Connor himself is unrecognizable: waist-deep in sludge, his eyebrows and mustache blackened with flecks of mud, his chest sifted with shining sediment. There is a branch in his hair.

A clap of thunder breaks the night air in two, releasing the downpour. Connor leaps out of the water and scrambles into the boat. He pulls on his jeans. Rain is plastering Lilly's cotton dress to the spheres of her body. The pressure on her skin feels good, so good she feels laughter bubbling up from inside her. The image of Connor waist-deep in the lake is etched on her retinas like a photographic negative.

"Here." He arranges his shirt in a tent over her hair and shoulders. She holds it tightly shut at her chin as though it was a veil.

"Peas!" he crows as he rows back to shore. "We're going to have so many goddamn peas, Newman, you're going to have to teach that girl how to can!"

"Freeze," Lilly says. "You don't can peas, you freeze them. It's easy."

It seems only a minute before they have reached the shore and Connor is helping Lilly out of the wooden boat. "Go slow," she says, hooking one hand in his belt loop to steady herself as they start up the hill in the dark. The rain is slapping against his bare back; she holds his shirt closed at her chin. She wonders if it's odd that there is no one in the world she trusts like she trusts Connor.

At the top of the hill, two rectangles of lamplight fall through the cabin windows onto the wet grass, their geometry interrupted only by the silhouette of Kaitlin's shoulders hunched in worry at the screen. Lilly releases Connor's belt loop and they walk separately into the light.

"Stranger in Paradise"

"Catastrophe!" Estelle Mundy gasped as her long pale pianist's fingers placed the seven of spades between the two red jacks. Her neck and forehead burned. The small of her back felt weak. She dropped the rest of the deck on the breakfast table and scurried in her sideways fashion to the sink for a little confidence. The house was empty now, but it was still her policy to take up as little room as possible as she moved about. From the cabinet under the sink she retrieved a family-size box of Tide, empty except for her confidence. She looked at her wristwatch. Ten after ten. With a deliciously personal sense of defeat, she poured and downed two shots. She waited with the cap off and her hand on the neck of the bottle to see if two would do the trick. The rosy vodka calm spread through her head. Her lips settled in an ambiguous half-smile.

Estelle was forty-two. She was slight. Her figure was not memorable. The last five years had seen her pageboy turn from chestnut brown to pewter gray. Her countenance, her bearing—everything about her was mild. Everything but her eyes. They were huge, excitable eyes, silver in color. Like sudden pools of feeling, they lay in her face, waiting to be tripped over. For as long as Estelle could remember, her eyes had seen things that nobody else in Clarity, Iowa, had seen.

The sound of footsteps on the back porch startled her. It wasn't her father. The Reverend Mundy was in St. Louis, receiving an award at the Methodist Ministers' Convention. Estelle poured and downed another shot. The oval doorknob rattled as it turned. "Who is it?" she called. She slipped the friendly bottle back in the box and tucked the wild orange flap in place. "Who else!" she muttered, affecting an offhand stance as Opal Turk poked her head in the kitchen. Opal was a rotund, red-faced woman who lived next door, which entitled her, she felt, to walk in without knocking.

"Didn't catch you doing something nasty, did I?" Opal said. She always said that and then she always added, "Of course not." She raised an eyebrow at the cards laid out in fortune-telling formation on the table. "Humid for October, ain't it?" was all she said.

Estelle hurried over to the table and sat down on top of the cards to cover them up. "Very close," she agreed. "But I imagine those shorts of yours keep you cool. Can you buy that size at Waddington's?"

Opal ignored the question. She stood stock-still and locked her arms in place over her chest. "You're not busy practicing, are you?" she said. Estelle's much-publicized "Night of Chopin" to benefit the new hospital wing was scheduled to take place in three days. KRIT was bringing it live to several hundred thousand listeners. The ambitious program was to be performed on a concert grand being shipped to Clarity for the occasion, courtesy of the Masonic Lodge. It was on its way now.

"Busy isn't even the word," Estelle said.

"Well, don't let me keep you." Opal marched over to the sink and opened the cabinets, upper and lower. Through an effort of will, Estelle stayed where she was, hatching the jacks and the seven.

"Where do you keep your water glasses?" Opal asked.

"Right door, middle shelf, where they've been for forty years."

Opal glugged down a jelly glass of water. "That was quite an old picture of yourself you gave the *Des Moines Register*," she said. The statewide newspaper had published a long interview with Estelle in its Sunday magazine. "The cultural anomaly of northern Iowa," they dubbed her.

Estelle glared at Opal. "It said, 'Mundy in Drake days,'" she quoted. "Don't you read captions?"

"You're not the only one around here who's busy," Opal said. She rinsed the water glass out as slowly as possible to annoy Estelle.

"Nice of you to drop by," Estelle snapped. Opal pushed the fruit magnets on the refrigerator into a tight bunch and glanced at the cards peeking from beneath Estelle before she departed.

When the back door was shut again, Estelle reread the *Register* article her father had taped to the kitchen wall. She knew most of it by heart. Her favorite part was when the reporter asked her the secret to playing Chopin. "The longing in Chopin must be personal," Estelle had answered. "Some people say Chopin's muse was his twelve-year-old cousin, whom he loved but was forbidden to marry. If, indeed, he composed his music to reach one person, then it should be performed that way. It should sound as if it was played for one person."

The one person Estelle played for was Milo Creszick, former choral director of the Drake University School of Music in Des Moines. She had located him through the cards. He now lived in Seattle, and he had never married. The "Night of Chopin" was conceived to change all that. Estelle had mailed him the interview anonymously. She read the rest of the page. Imagining his eyes touching these black letters, she was overwhelmed with emotion.

Estelle raised her arms, chanteuse-style. "Take my haaaa-aaaaand," she sang boldly, advancing on tiptoe across the kitchen. She swirled around and backed up against the refrigerator with shivery, victimy shoulders. "I'm a stranger in para-diiiiiiise." Her voice cracked.

She got out the Tide and poured herself a water glass full of vodka. She took little swallows until the glass was empty. Then she repeated the procedure. When she looked at her watch it was ten to two. It looked exactly like ten after ten. Estelle hoped this was not going to be one of those afternoons when she started seeing things and then passed out. She had a lot to do. She hadn't practiced the piano in five years. She had three days to do the impossible: learn three sonatas, two études, seven mazurkas, the *Fantaisie*, and the *Polonaise*. The threat of exposure and humiliation was unbearable. That was the catastrophe.

Estelle decided to stop procrastinating right that minute. She dragged herself into the parlor and confronted her cherry-

wood upright. The Schirmer edition of the *Fantaisie* stood un-
opened on the music rack. She seated herself at the piano. The
front of her dress was sticking to her skin. She shook it wildly.
"No funny business, please, Fred," she said, addressing the
plaster-of-paris bust of Chopin sitting atop the upright. She
turned to page one and lifted her hands to the keyboard.

At four, Estelle picked out the melody to "What a Friend We
Have in Jesus." She'd been playing popular tunes by ear for
months, but neither her mother nor her father had noticed.
They were caught up in the tap dancing of Estelle's perfect
older sister, Mary Amaryllis. Besides, they didn't know any
popular tunes.

Estelle's desire for a baby sister "to be better than" was not
fulfilled when Father adopted the Gertz girls. Patty Lee Gertz
was sexy and Geraldine Gertz was morose. Their parents had
died in a fire. After Father announced his intentions to Estelle
and Mary Amaryllis, he ordered them never to refer to the lost
parents as trash again.

"Do we have to walk to school with them?" Mary Amaryllis
asked.

"Yes. We will love them as if they were our own."

"Where will they sleep?" Estelle asked. Father, Mother, and
Mary Amaryllis all looked at her. "Oh," Estelle said.

She couldn't study with two new adopted sisters listening to
the radio in her room, so she moved her desk into the tiny
gabled passageway that led to the attic. It was referred to as
Molly's room, after the farm girl who had stayed there to help
Mother during childbirth. When Estelle studied in Molly's
room, she could see things coming and going from the attic.

Soon she had isolated two very different ghosts. The downstairs ghost was dull. All he did was move the turquoise glass
peacock from one side of the television set to the other. Estelle
had always thought it was Mother doing that, but she caught
the ghost at it one Sunday night when she played sick from
Christian Youth Meeting to watch Loretta Young. The upstairs

ghost was whimsical and unpredictable, flashing the upstairs lights off and on, filling the bathtub with water when no one but Estelle was home, hiding her Sunday shoes in humorous places, like on top of Father's framed print of the Sermon on the Mount. Her sisters didn't believe her.

No one believed her until she found Darrell Wangler's missing IRS refund through the cards. She was playing solitaire. Father was trying to calm Darrell over the phone. Darrell was upset because all his bills, including his pledge to the Methodist church, would have to wait ninety days for the government to replace the refund. Turning over two threes and two sevens, Estelle could see that the check was still in its envelope in the middle of a book. Word spread when Darrell found the money in the Clarity Library's copy of *How Green Was My Valley*. He had used it as a bookmark. People began to come to Estelle regularly for help in finding their lost things. It made the Reverend Mundy fume. He didn't like the look in Estelle's eyes when she did the cards. It seemed heretical. He asked her to stop and she did.

Until she went to Drake. She went to Drake on a scholarship, and she figured that allowed her some leeway with Father's prejudices. The cards made her immensely popular, and popularity became her. Milo fell in love with her. He was a Polish refugee. He was bold, racy, impulsive. He waved his arms around passionately when he directed the chorus. The sight of the hair under his arms made Estelle sing as loud and high as a diva. She had never met such an exceptional, sensitive man. In his homeland, he was considered a genius. In Estelle's house, he was considered a Catholic. The Reverend Mundy had forbidden Estelle to dance with Catholics.

After rehearsals, Estelle would be very slow to put her music away. When she was the last student in the room, she would look at Milo and he would follow her into the oaken cloakroom. She would lower her eyes and he would dress her for the cold—cape, scarf, hat, and mittens. Then at the thought of saying good-bye until the next meeting of the chorus, they would kiss. Soon they would be thrashing about on the floor, Estelle feverish in her hot outerwear. A streetlamp shone through the high barred window. Stripes of darkness fell on their faces, making them strangers to each other.

Her senior year, Estelle began to concentrate on the works of Chopin for her piano recital. Milo gave her the plaster-of-paris bust for her birthday. He would sit in on her rehearsals and cry. She thought it was because of her technique, but it wasn't: he was tired of disposing of his desire alone in his apartment after their sessions in the cloakroom. Milo had gotten a Guggenheim. He asked Estelle to go to Paris with him in the fall. She decided to ask her father for permission to marry him. If he refused, they would elope.

Estelle went home at Easter break to sound Father out. He was too busy the first few days to see her. Playing solitaire secretly in Molly's room, Estelle saw in the two black queens that her mother had started to die. She gathered her sisters together and whispered the horrid truth. They reported her to the Reverend. He called Estelle into his study and took away her cards. It was hardly an opportune moment to ask permission to marry a Catholic. She would try again in August.

In August, the Reverend's wife was yellow. The diagnosis was kidney disease. Everyone hung their heads when Father made the announcement. Mother would have to be driven to Des Moines to the dialysis machine three times a week. Someone would have to stay home and tend to her needs. Patty Lee burst into tears.

"I'm pregnant," she sobbed. "I didn't want to trouble you with wedding plans."

The Reverend swallowed hard. His eyes offered comfort only out of habit. "You shall have a real wedding," he said, "as if you were one of my own."

"Then I'm getting married now too," Mary Amaryllis said. "I'm not waiting for a year. In a year Mother might be green. Or dead."

Nobody looked at Geraldine. Geraldine was moping around

the parsonage all day chain-smoking. She had just gotten an interview for a job at the Maytag factory in Newton. Everyone wanted her out of the house. They all looked at Estelle.

"Oh," Estelle said. The image of Milo's chest hair climbing out of his shirt in the striped darkness of the cloakroom flashed in her brain, causing her secret embarrassment. She told Milo the elopement would have to wait. Seven days later, he went to Paris alone.

The Reverend Mundy's sermons demanded more and more faith of his congregation. Estelle tried to be the first to give him measurable results. She volunteered for the job of organist for both the nine and the eleven o'clock services. Brilliant, crystal-clear Bach and great, tormented Beethoven rained down on the ears of the farmers and merchants every Sunday in the Methodist church. They began to send their daughters and sons to Estelle after school to learn to play. Once in a while, when they lost something precious—a gold ring, prescription sunglasses—they would ask Estelle privately to do the cards. She wanted to mind her father perfectly. She refused. She considered it all temporary. No one knew Mother would hang on for fifteen years.

Opal Turk had three tone-deaf children, but her niece, Darlene, had perfect pitch. Darlene was not a born musician, but she could easily be developed into a small-town organist if she continued to practice diligently for Estelle. Darlene's lesson was every Tuesday at four-thirty. Estelle was surprised when she showed up one Thursday night at eleven, pale and shaking, accompanied by her aunt. Darlene had won the bingo jackpot—a hundred and forty dollars—at the Catholic church next door to the parsonage. She had put the cash in her purse. Now it was missing.

Darlene asked Estelle to find it. "I told her," Opal said, "you promised your father not to do the cards. A promise is a promise." She shrugged.

Estelle was outraged. She did not need the cards to find the ten missing tens and two missing twenties, but she reached for her deck anyway. "Commitment to a principle sometimes includes abandoning it," she said simply.

Opal looked as if her face would burst. She clutched her ruby plastic pocketbook. Estelle turned over the first card, a ten. She completed the formation, dealing the cards face down into a cross around the ten, then turning over the top four cards. Opal was twitching.

"Oh, dear," Estelle said.

"Where?" Darlene begged.

Estelle focused her silver eyes on Opal.

"Aunt Opal!" Darlene gasped. "I wouldn't lend it to you, so you took it!" She grabbed at Opal's purse, but Opal swatted her with it.

"Girls!" Estelle cried.

Opal and Darlene were deadlocked with all four hands on the pocketbook. They fell to the floor and wrestled around on the living room rug. The peacock slid off the television and crashed to the floor. Now the downstairs ghost would have nothing to do. Darlene finally got the pocketbook away from Opal, opened it, and dumped out the money.

"Now look what you've done!" Opal shouted at Estelle. "The work of the devil!"

"Opal has been punished enough," the Reverend Mundy said a week later, when the story was all over town. He placed his hand baptismally on his second daughter's head. "Go to her and ask her forgiveness for your part in it. Rise above her wrong."

Estelle was speechless.

"For my sake," Mrs. Mundy called from her sickbed in the solarium. "Even as ye do it unto the least of these, ye do it unto Me."

Squeezed between the twisted logic of Father and the martyrdom of Mother, Estelle felt like she used to when they tricked her into sitting in the front seat of the car between their big elbows while Mary Amaryllis stretched out in back to get her beauty rest. "I can't," she said.

"Do you know in your heart that you did the right thing?" asked the Reverend.

"Yes."

"Then you are free to take the first step. We must always set an example of generosity."

"I always have," Estelle said. Apparently Father had not kept track of all that she had given up. He smiled condescendingly.

"It is testimony to our selfishness that our few small deeds seem like immense compromises. Go to Opal. You will see how transforming an act of love can be."

Estelle was baffled. She crossed the driveway and stood at Opal's back door. She knocked. When Opal opened the door, Estelle, to her surprise, punched her in the jaw.

Her sisters discussed it privately when they gathered at the parsonage for Mother's funeral a week later. None of them took Estelle's side. They were suspicious of the way the card activity was tied up with Mother's death. People in town began to whisper that maybe Estelle should have moved out on her own a long, long time ago.

These things Estelle could have taken in her stride. It was Father's coldness that tipped the scales. He barely spoke to her. She began to sit through her rehearsal time in the dark nave of the Methodist church with her bottle of confidence. On Sunday mornings she faked the organ offertory for both services. She had intended to do it only once, to get back at the congregation for not sticking up for her, but when no one complained she did it again out of curiosity. The third time she did it undetected, she realized with despair that all those years they had never really known when she had played well.

Estelle had not been able to sight-read all the way through the *Fantaisie*. Her hands were shaky and sloppy from the alcohol. As a last resort, she decided to run through the heart-breaker, the Tenth Etude. The folio binding was long gone. The pages were loaded with emphasis marks from her college days. The fingers of her right hand moved from one key to the next, and the familiar melody filled the parlor. Pure, chaste, and sweet with longing, it was the cousin line. Below in the left hand, rich, rolling chords rumbled with Slavic desire. Gradually the right-hand melody, as if frustrated that it would never get to be with the left hand, began to embroider itself with worried little flourishes. As the frenzy grew, the flourishes multiplied into chords. Mounting to a climax, the two hands seemed deceptively united. But the more the keyboard rang with sound, the more the sweet melody, the forbidden loved one, was lost forever.

Sweat poured off Estelle's hands as she turned the last page. The black notes seemed to collect in clusters that looked like the seven of spades. She wiped her hands quickly on her lap and pounded the étude to its conclusion. The final lifting of the pedal swallowed up the music and left the parlor hollow.

"If only they all came that easy," she whispered to Chopin. There was a loud banging noise. "Don't let me down now, Fred," Estelle begged. "Please be a good boy and we'll try the mazurkas." She reached for the folio. The banging continued, like someone was hammering on the air conditioner.

Estelle thought she saw large hailstones all over the parson-age lawn. Her head filled with a roaring sound—as if the Rock Island Railroad was steaming through her house, as if she was passing out. "Stop it!" she ordered Chopin. The lights flashed off and on, then went out.

The room seemed to rise up and spin around slowly like a merry-go-round. Through the parlor window, Estelle saw the Luicks' roof fly off and Dotty's china cabinet sail out of the dining room—all the plates were still behind the rack. She saw the hundred pipes of the Methodist church organ go whirling upward into the sky. She saw Opal's white Mustang jump backward into the air and hit a telephone pole. Before anything else could happen, Estelle grabbed Chopin by the throat and hurled him out the bay window, which she forgot was closed.

As he crashed through the glass, every window in the parsonage exploded, making a sound like five thousand crystal goblets smashing in a bathtub. Estelle's ears popped. The room fell. The sky was black and it was pouring rain. Estelle was confused. She couldn't find the door so she climbed out the window.

Electric lines were lying in menacing coils all over the street. Trees were broken off at the trunks. People were running up and down the street yelling that the downtown was in shambles. Mary Meservey was pulling at the door of a car smashed by a brick chimney. "Someone's in there!" she was crying.

Estelle hoped someone would help Mary, because she couldn't. Her attention was entirely drawn to a single layer of bright yellow apples arranged in a perfect circle in the middle of the parsonage lawn. She had planted a Grimes Golden there when Mother died. The tornado had ripped the tree from the earth and funneled it God knew where. Estelle was sure that the ripe fruit had been delicately left behind out of respect for her mother. She collected the golden apples carefully in the drenched skirt of her dress.

"Take twenty cups of corn," said Helen Caine, "fresh off the cob. Stir it together with a pound of melted oleo and a cup of milk. Put it in the oven in a big roasting pan for an hour at three hundred. Stir it once or twice. Let it cool. Freeze it. That's it!"

"It tastes fresh!" Estelle said. She and Helen were having lunch in the makeshift hospital dormitory that the Red Cross had set up in the high school. Everyone was grateful the high school was still standing. Estelle found the dorm food delicious. Today, Helen's corn and beef stew were on the menu.

Helen had donated the contents of her freezer to the relief effort. Her eyes were swathed in cotton. A sycamore tree had fallen into her sewing room while she was putting an appliqué on an apron. Both eyes were badly scratched. She relied on Estelle to describe the movements of the injured in and out of the dorm. Estelle liked Helen's company. She liked the crisp hospital sheets. She liked drying out. She continued to complain of elusive back pain so she wouldn't be sent home.

"Do you know what they said at the station house?" she asked Helen.

"No, what?"

"They said they saw the tornado scoop the water out of the Iowa River. When they looked, the riverbed was dry. What I want to know is, where did the water go?"

"I haven't the slightest idea," Helen said.

"I know where my organ went. It went straight up. I saw it."

"There'll be no concert on that organ!" Helen said with authority.

"No concert at all!" Estelle concurred. She didn't bother to correct Helen. Let her think Chopin wrote for the organ. The Ruan truck bearing the concert grand had long since returned to Des Moines. The whole hospital had been destroyed. There was no point in promoting a wing. Estelle was saved.

"Maynard's bed is still empty," she reported, craning her neck. "It doesn't look good." Maynard Axelrod was the postman. In the house-to-house search conducted by the National Guard during the first twenty-four hours after the tornado, Maynard did not turn up. His family begged Estelle to find him. She did the cards right there in the makeshift hospital. "He's at the intersection of Railroad and Southwest Third Street," she said.

They found him wrapped up in a piece of corrugated aluminum siding ripped off the soybean plant. The siding, with Maynard in it, was wound around a telephone pole. "Do you know what he said to his neighbor when he came to?" Estelle asked Helen.

"No, what?"

"He said, 'Clive, does your dog still brush his teeth?'"

Helen laughed. "That's not funny."

When the lunch trays were cleared, Estelle asked a volunteer to help her lie down. "Hand this to Mrs. Caine, please," she instructed.

"What is it?" Helen asked, feeling around the edges of a block of wood.

"Feel in the middle," Estelle directed.

"Feathers!" Helen exclaimed, stroking the soft strands protruding from both surfaces of the board.

"It's one feather," Estelle explained. "It's one feather stuck in the middle of a piece of pine. It wasn't blown straight in either. The tornado unwound the grain of the wood and the feather sailed in. Then the grain snapped back around it."

"Who would think it!"

Helen was smiling and stroking the feather like a cat's tail. "It's white," Estelle said. She smiled too. She felt lighter than air. All the older people—arthritics, asthmatics, rheumatics— were reporting an unexpected reprieve from their discomforts. The tornado had rearranged the ions in the atmosphere with its vacuum. People had never felt so good.

Estelle knew it was temporary, but she wanted to enjoy every minute of it. She felt under her pillow to make sure that the letter from Milo was still there. She closed her eyes and waited for the afternoon mail, even though it was too soon to expect an answer to her reply.

The Sad-Womb Son

A woman has two sons she loves equally. One is born at a happy time, one at a sad time. The happy-womb son likes to talk. He talks incessantly, the only time he is not talking is when he is listening. The woman answers all his questions. The sad-womb son is quiet. He likes to build and destroy. He makes whimsical things, useful things, obtrusive things.

They live in a little house in Scataway, a town in New Jersey, next to a park with a small woods. The three of them are close—so close that the woman's husband brings a kitten home for himself.

The woman begins to notice something. Maybe she's sweeping the walk, maybe she's stirring the stew—suddenly she realizes that her sad-womb son has been talking and she hasn't heard a word. "Why?" he wants to know and waits for her answer. She asks him to repeat his question. She vows to listen, she struggles to keep her vow, but even as he speaks some muffled blankness fills her ears. He asks her why a second time and she can't answer. Her desk at the furniture factory is decorated with things built by him; she keeps his photograph by her bed, though he is right down the hall. Some part of her is afraid of losing him, but it is the happy-womb son she loses.

He was last seen wearing his favorite purple sneakers, his jacket covered with astronaut patches from the Air and Space Museum. He was carrying a lunch box. His eyes were blue. His hair was light brown. His birthday was 4/12/72. He was standing on the usual corner waiting for the school bus. He was on time; the sad-womb son was late.

The kind man at the Foundation to Find America's Children files a report; he sends out an all-points bulletin that will be picked up by any state law enforcement agency equipped with a Teletype; he enters the happy-womb son under Missing Persons in the FBI's computer. Eight days go by. The woman walks into the path of a car, cuts off the tip of her finger with a bread knife, burns half her hair lighting a cigarette. "We've got to do more," she tells the kind man, her face inches from his face.

She can feel her happy-womb son alive in the world some-where; her blood flows in his direction. She quits her job to help the kind man find her son. He understands—he's trained to expect a stage like this from a woman like her.

Three years go by. The New Jersey police are tired of the woman. She has drained her friends dry, they're afraid of her now. Her husband has gone to live by himself in an apartment nearby. Her sad-womb son runs away from home, but in a few hours he comes back. The woman is poison, infecting every-one. Only the kind man is still kind. Photos of the happy-womb son are on milk cartons and cat litter bags, though there is too much ink in his eyes. Twice, calls reporting him have come in; twice, the kind man has taken the woman to look at boys who were not her son. Driving home, she wanted to hurt the kind man. He understood—he was trained to expect it.

The woman sometimes tortures herself with his statistics. She knows, for example, how many unidentified bodies per year turn up that are nine or ten years old. She knows what the odds are that her son is alive; if he is alive, she knows what is probably being done to him and by whom. The purple sneakers are long gone. So are the astronaut patches. Her son has changed. She cannot feel him in her blood. Alive or dead, he's different. To whom does she pray about this and how?

Four years have gone by. The woman is a walled scream. She has her job back; she sweeps the walk, she stirs the stew. Thirty-five thousand hours have been logged on her case. One spring day she spades up the earth behind her insignificant house. A wail is heard. The woman straightens her back to listen. The wail is repeated over and over, always beginning on the same wild, sharp note. It sounds like a baby crying. A scuttering in the bushes near the woods draws her attention.

Her estranged husband's cat, a sweet tabby, emerges from the woods with a baby rabbit hanging from her jaws. The cat sits, her eyes blank as she patiently severs the jugular. No noise comes from the rabbit, though his hind legs gallop in place.

The wail continues in the woods, always on the same wild note: it's not a baby crying at all—it's a mother. The eyes of the baby grow peaceful and still; his legs bound ever more confidently in place. He thinks he's safe, he thinks he's free, he thinks he's home. What he thinks is all that matters. The woman wants to tell the mother rabbit this.

She lies down in the dirt of the garden. She rubs her hands in it and licks her fingertips. It tastes bitter, but she likes the texture against her teeth, gritty, grainy. She sits up, then stands up and walks into her house. She wants to trust nature. Long ago she had that trust. She wants it back.

A few months later, the woman contributes to the newsletter at work. Someone asks her to bowl and she goes. By Thanksgiving, she thinks she is ready to go to her rich sister's home in Washington, D.C., where all the astronaut patches were purchased. She and her sad-womb son board the train in Trenton, early, the day before the holiday. He is twelve, he gets the window. At every station, the train is delayed while people push aboard with luggage and presents. They press down the aisles, brushing the woman's cheek with harsh coat sleeves, bumping her knees with boxes. Slowly the cars fill, until there's a person in every seat.

The woman watches her son write a few words in a blue pocket notebook. His chin is nicely shaped, his hair darker than she remembers. She tries to read his writing without his noticing. *Why*, she reads, *do people*—something. Tangle? *Travel. On holidays? Why don't they stay where they are?* He pauses, wondering. The hind end of Delaware lurches by the window. *They need to get back*, he writes. *To their group. Because of the food? Yes. No one wants to eat alone. It doesn't taste right. The group makes the food taste good. They remember. They*—something. Argue? *Agree. If it tasted good alone, no one would move. Everyone would stay where they are, like stones. Why isn't it like that?* The woman wonders this herself.

She admires his clean hands. How has he learned to clip his

nails? How has he become all this without her help? She has forgotten to raise him, yet he has never left her side except that once, and then he came back.

The woman taps her son's arm. He turns. She asks him if he wants to play the old guessing game they used to play on trips. He wants to. He plays well, better than her—she starts acting silly. He could win every turn, but he doesn't—he wants to make sure she will ask him to play again.

The woman can't sleep that night—she is too happy. All the next day, whenever she wishes someone a Happy Thanksgiving, she gets a lump in her throat. The sound of the word "happy" makes her feel they're all together again.

Likely Houses

Alice and Willie owned a saltbox shack on the edge of an onion field in upstate New York. They had bought it for next to nothing with every intention of fixing it up. Once in a while, Willie would measure a broken window for glass or drive into Gardnerville for a floorboard, but mostly the task of making the shack into a home like Alice claimed she was used to overwhelmed him and he ignored it.

Alice resigned herself to the debris more successfully as a young wife than as a young mother. Cooped up all day, nursing and changing William, she found that she could vent her fury at her plain surroundings only by imagining things that weren't true. One of the things she would imagine as she sat in her Leatherette kitchen chair—looking out the west window at the wooded hill half a mile across the onion field—was that she lived in the little red house at the top of the hill. It seemed to sit there, the house, in a circle of green and Alice wanted some green around her. She wanted more than furrows and onion tops. She wanted a lawn.

There was a plain dirt plot out the west window littered with Willie's junk. It could have become a lawn, but circumstances had combined to make the transformation impossible that spring. First, Alice found out she was pregnant again. That meant she would be too tired to seed the plot all by herself. Second, Willie got laid off at the garage. That meant there would be no money. Alice found this hard to accept. Frustration rose in her passive gray eyes and molded her usually mild, indefinite features into a forward-moving face, like the front of a well-designed car.

One April day when the sky was steadily sifting rain, Alice stood at her post by the front door watching for Ray to bring the mail. William was in the process of learning how to open the cabinet under the sink, take out all the pots and pans, and bang the lids together like cymbals. "Cripes," muttered Alice, putting her hands over her ears to block out the noise.

"Shut that kid up!" Willie shouted from his chair where he was watching TV commercials. "I can't hear nothing."

"You shut him up!" Alice shouted back. "I'm waiting for the mailman."

"That's not doing nothing," Willie argued.

"If you'd fix the goddamn mailbox so's it wouldn't let the rain ruin the newspaper, maybe you'd have some peace and quiet." He answered her by turning the TV all the way up. When Ray's mail truck pulled up in front, she ran out into the rain, slamming the front door as hard as she could.

"Wet enough for you?" Ray smiled.

"It may be wet, but it don't talk back," Alice huffed. He laughed and drove off. There was nothing to speak of in the mail besides the newspaper. Alice sat in her Leatherette chair and read the want ads with a vengeance until the noise level made her cry. She took the lids away from William and put him in his playpen. He screamed bloody murder. She stuck him in the high chair and put a stack of saltines in front of him. "Always getting your way, aren't you?" she said wearily. While he ate, she turned her back and gazed out the window at the plot.

It would be all picked up, all cleaned up, no car parts, no tools, no toys, no broken rocker, no inner tube. It would be lush and uniform with sweet, bright green grass drinking up the April rain. There would be marigolds in a corner bed and pansies in front and gladiolas in back. There would be a white birdbath on a fluted pedestal and one new white lawn chair— her chair. It would be her room. A place she could go.

As she gazed, the baby kicked inside her belly. "Ow!" she laughed. "Well, there you are, aren't you? It's about time!" She pressed the place on her belly where the kick had come and smiled. "Willie!" she called. "The baby kicked!" She ran in to tell him since he couldn't hear. It was the kind of thing he wanted to know.

"That's my punter!" Willie grinned. "I got a linebacker, now

I want a punter! And then we'll just keep right on making them until we got us a whole team. Best team in the world!" He leaned back in his lounge chair and beamed at her proudly. Alice beamed back. She did not remind him that it was her turn to have a girl. There were fewer and fewer moments when Willie was proud. Pride made his baby face cute again, like it was in high school.

"Willie," she said suddenly, "should I get a job?"

He turned the TV down. "Alice," he said, "we've been over this before. Number 1, you can't do nothing but clean house, and I won't have you doing that in your condition. Number 2, all we got is the tow truck. If you did work, how would you get there? You can't drive my tow truck. I might get a call and then I'm making money. Number 3, name one outfit in this country which hires a woman who they know from the outset will quit in three, four months and never come back." He bent forward and increased the volume.

"There is one ad," Alice raised her voice, "for a part-time representative." She found it hard to take a stand against him.

"Part-time representative," she quoted from the paper, "demonstrate educational materials. No experience necessary. Guaranteed $$ per week."

Willie guffawed. "You are so naive! You don't know what that is?"

"What is it?"

"Encyclopedia salesman."

"Oh, no," Alice whimpered. Her face fell. Willie was so knowledgeable. "Why do they call it by another name?"

He laughed again. "Call the number, go ahead. See if I'm right."

"You hold William then," she said, "so I can hear myself think." She wiped the cracker mess from the creases of William's fat hands and plopped him down in Willie's lap. She took the phone into the kitchen as far as the cord would allow. When she returned in fifteen minutes, Willie had forgotten all about their discussion. "I'm doing it!" she announced confidently.

He scowled at her for a moment, alarmed by her unusually triumphant manner. When he realized what she was talking about he grumbled, "Over my dead body!"

"I've met all your criteria," Alice said, using the lady on the phone's phrase.

"Already she's talking funny," Willie said to William. They both looked up at her with sweet, demanding expressions.

"Number 1, they train you," Alice said, pressing her index fingers together chest-high in a list-making gesture. She talked rapidly and her usual lack of logic was not in evidence. "Number 2, for the first four weeks someone will be able to pick me up and take me home. After that, I'm on my own and I can go out as little as once a week. You can give me that tow truck once a week, Willie, *one morning.* Number 3, I can quit anytime to have the baby and come back to work when I feel ready."

Willie looked hurt. His eyes retreated and his jaw set the way it did when his mother was coming over. "Who is *they?*" he asked. "It better not be a *he.*"

"*They* is Barbara Canter, the regional director of Universal Knowledge." Willie shook his head. "Well?" Alice asked after a long pause.

"Well, what?" Willie said. His voice sounded tired.

"Well, can I? She's on the phone."

"Got to be fancy, don't you?" he chided, drawing it out. "Got to be like Carol June and get a job. Well, I'm telling you, Alice, you ain't no Carol June. Carol June's got no family and Carol June's got no heart. You got both. You can't make it out there. You start exposing yourself to those elements and they'll eat you up. You won't even know what hit you. People will walk all over you, Alice Ann."

"Well, then you'd have some company, wouldn't you?" Alice hissed. "Look, Willie, I want a lawn." She put her hands on her hips and bent forward a little to make her point. "I want myself a real grass lawn. I want to sit on it *this* summer with my new baby. You ain't working and you can't give it to me. I don't hold it against you. But don't you hold it against me that I want it."

"Alice Ann, if you get one scratch on that tow truck," Willie pointed his index finger right at her heart, "and I mean a *scratch*, you'll never drive it again. You'll never even sit in it. You'll *walk* to the frigging hospital."

"It's a deal!" Alice snapped. She picked up the phone and said with a quaver in her voice, "Barbara? What time tonight?"

Barbara's home was color-coordinated. It was the only Tudor home in Gardnerville. It had framed pictures from Italy and a grand piano. Barbara's husband, Alberto, traveled to New York City to sing in the opera. Everyone was lucky to be in her home, since this was Barbara's last class. She was being promoted and would be leaving the area with Alberto in a few months. Alice sat on the white sofa with a glass coffee cup and saucer in her lap, feeling awkward and out of place.

"It's a lovely, lovely color," someone named Millie was saying ingratiatingly to Barbara about the french blue carpeting. "What kind of backing does it have?"

"Jute!" Barbara enunciated enthusiastically. She stood before her class, statuesque and energetic in her pastel double-knit suit. She started all her sentences by raising her eyebrows dramatically and widening her eyes. Her manner dispelled any urge to gossip among the five trainees. The gave her their undivided attention as she led them through the Six Steps to a Super Sale. At the end, she held up an order blank. "Every time you get one of these signed, you're closing a deal: it's thirty-five dollars in your pocket. Beginners close one out of every five presentations. And that's not just a statistic—it's history!" People's backs straightened. They had a hell of a company behind them. "Watch closely now," Barbara said, "at this special training film. Lights!" Trainees at either end of the white sofa reached for the table lamp switches.

Alice, who felt exaggeratedly empowered by Barbara's

speaking voice, almost immediately went into a daze as the staticky music of the sound track began to waver in the darkened living room. She spent the whole twenty minutes wondering what jute was, where Barbara's husband hid during the training sessions, what a black projector would look like in her own living room, and other things that she really couldn't ask at the question-and-answer period which followed the film.

Suddenly everyone was standing up and saying good night. "Practice the Six Steps to a Super Sale at home this week on your husbands," Barbara said in closing. "They'll tease you at first, but that's men."

Gardnerville was a humdrum, economically depressed burg in which five of the six main county roads uneventfully converged. It had functioned for Alice as a stern, reproving municipality which withheld things from her family—jobs, food, shoes, clothing, Congoleum, dishwashers, roofing shingles, patio tiles, and driveway shale. Now it became demystified: it was a territory. Alice and Barbara would cruise around side streets and back roads in Barbara's bronze Oldsmobile, looking for likely houses. A likely house had swing sets in back and bikes or trikes in front. Aboveground pools or cars in the driveway were also good signs.

They would call on likely houses until Barbara could demonstrate a complete presentation for Alice, sniffing out and avoiding the deadly stallers ("They'll yes you through the whole Six Steps before admitting they can't sign anything without their husbands"). Three out of five times, Barbara would close a sale. There was a great feeling of exhilaration at a closing. If there was no closing, Alice and Barbara would pad politely back to the Oldsmobile, giggling at the way the wife ate a Cheerio off the kitchen floor or the husband's toupee kept slipping forward.

Alice began to resent going home to her own unlikely house. Instead of being proud, Willie was jealous. His complaints would come hurling at her the minute she stepped in the door. "You're late! What's for dinner? Your kid never shut up this morning. He crapped all over the hall. Where'd you put my socks? Didn't you do a laundry yet? Take this brat off my hands—I want a nap."

Alice would stomp around fuming, cramming laundry into the machine, slamming dishes, feeding snotty William, vacuuming up Willie's inconsiderate mud. She never had time to sit in her Leatherette chair and imagine things. She began to want a husband who was more like Barbara.

The day before Alice was to go out on her own in the tow truck for the first time, Willie got especially pigheaded. He blasted her with his "you can't do nothing but clean house" speech, but he couldn't make her cry. She didn't believe him anymore. She drifted upstairs and lay naked on the white sheets, her arms around her unborn baby, until the fragile May dusk gathered in the uncurtained window.

Stirred to remorse by a made-for-TV movie, Willie climbed the stairs at ten o'clock and stood in the doorway. "Why am I the dumb one?" he whispered. "You got it all. You got the smarts and you get to have the babies too. What do I get?" Alice crumbled into tiny tears like dew.

It was a delirious May morning. The clouds were voluptuous. Lilac smell—so strong it seemed cheap—wafted over from the house next door. Alice crossed herself for good luck—something she hadn't done since high school. She forced herself up into the cab of the tow truck with her UK briefcase. In order to reach the pedals with her feet, she had to push her belly up against the steering wheel.

Alice drove straight to Heritage Hills, a new subdivision of split-level homes on the north side of Gardnerville. There she called on a Mr. LeVore, a widower working nights for the telephone company. He was just about to go to sleep. His living room floor was covered with asphalt linoleum because he had five sons. Mr. LeVore wanted Universal Knowledge for his sons, but his property taxes were going up in June and he wanted to see the bill before he bought anything new. He suggested Mrs. Riker across the street, who was Miss Poland in 1957 before she came to this country and married a Riker. Mrs. Riker was waxing her kitchen floor and asked Alice to come back in half an hour.

Alice called on a bright, talkative, chain-smoking lady named Benita who was too smart for her own good and figured out at Step Five of the Six Steps exactly how much Universal Knowledge would really cost her on the installment plan, including interest. Benita then tried to get Alice to take her commission off the selling price in exchange for three months of Nutrilife Vitamins, for which Benita was the county distributor. Fortunately, Alice left without ever knowing what Benita was talking about.

Down the street at a very likely house—new avocado appliances and a redwood deck—Alice almost made a double sale to two neighbors, Jean and Jenine. With identical hairdos, they sat together at the dining room table drooling over the offer Alice unfolded with her four-color poster. They were even planning to order the dictionary, the atlas, and the yearbooks when the phone rang. Alice listened, stunned, while Jean's mother talked her out of Universal Knowledge. "Mom's going to give me her old Britannica," Jean told Alice with a shrug.

"Then we can use it too!" Jenine said.

Alice was furious. She left Heritage Hills without going back to old Miss Poland and drove the fifteen miles back to her own neighborhood at sixty-five miles an hour. She needed one more complete presentation to make her quota of five. It was then that she thought of the red house on the hill. She swerved onto the access road and drove across the onion field. As the tow truck climbed the wooded hill, winding to the left and then to the right, every bump and stone in the road slammed the baby against Alice's bladder. Alice was terrified that she would pee in her pants. She tried all the old tricks, singing "Onward, Christian Soldiers," holding herself with one hand, picturing a toilet with the lid up waiting for her somewhere in the near future.

"This is not a likely house!" Alice announced, feeling deceived as she entered the grassy clearing at the top. All of her hopes fell at once. Only the front of the house was painted red and it was a bad red—somebody's leftover deck enamel. The whole clearing was deserted, except for an old woman sitting in a white rocker on the concrete stoop.

Alice waddled through the tickly meadow grass to the stoop. She said hello to the old lady and knocked on the door.

"Come in," the old lady said.

"Oh!" Alice said, turning to her again. "Do they have a bathroom I might use? I live down the hill, but I've been out making sales calls. Now I can't tell you how bad I have to go."

"Don't apologize," the old lady said. "Go on inside. It's on the left. Toilet don't flush, so take the pail and fill it with tap water and pour it down the stool after yourself."

Sun filled the bare bungalow, illuminating every inadequacy of style and comfort. Alice sat on the toilet feeling sorry for the old lady, who obviously lived completely alone. She looked out the bathroom window and saw the roof of her own house at the edge of the onion field. It looked fixed up from here. This enraged Alice because it wasn't fixed up. It wasn't fixed up at all.

"You come down and visit me someday," Alice said to the old lady on her way out.

"Oh, I'm not lonely!" She smiled. "I'm as busy as I could be!" Her face crinkled into a vibrant mask of joy. She gave the impression of perfect freedom, sailing serenely there in her white chair with no obstacles to her enjoyment. "I just rock and think, rock and think!"

"Well, if you ever *do* get lonely, you just come right on down," Alice repeated.

"Good luck with your sales." The old lady smiled.

"Well, you know, it takes two incomes these days," Alice

complained, "to get things done around the house and keep the family in shoes and whatnot."

"Don't worry about it," the old lady instructed. "It don't come to nothing anyway. All your wishing and wanting—it don't end up making any difference. Your hubby will die on you and your children will move to California like mine and all that will be left of your life is how much love you actually gave them."

Alice's features filled with hate. She smiled politely and left. Her teeth were gritting as she lunged back down the disappointing hill, and she took the final turn onto the access road at a defiant forty-five miles an hour. A huge green tiller clambered slowly out of the onion field into her path. She could scrape by if she kept going, but she would crease the whole right side of the tow truck. Willie would kill her. Summoning all of her being into a single column of prayer, she begged, "Please, God, not a scratch!" and slammed on the brakes. Her belly flew into the steering wheel. The horizon spun insanely in the windshield and when it stopped, it lay at a tilt. Alice opened her eyes. The front end of the truck was nose to nose with the tiller. The back wheel hung precariously over the drainage ditch.

The tiller's driver climbed out of his seat and stood looking at Alice. His mouth was a line that lay noncommittally in his face. He had the look of someone whose will had bent to the will of the sky again and again without breaking. He looked at Alice with admiration. It had been his assumption that the collision had been averted by a man, a better man than he, for his reflexes were slow and he knew it.

"My fault," he called, "can I do anything?"

In a loud, frustrated voice that echoed over the onion field, Alice cried, "Would you *please* buy a set of goddamn encyclopedias?"

He thought for a moment. His brother-in-law had just bought a set. His wife had been on him to get one. "Yes," he called back, "yes, I would."

Diamond Twill

It was inexplicable to Mr. and Mrs. Glen H. Purty that their twenty-three-year-old daughter, Crystal, wanted to leave her job as a computer programmer at Azcom Communications to be a weaver. She wanted to live off her savings. She wanted to give up her lavender bedroom in their lovely Montclair, New Jersey, home to live in an old house full of people who shared one bathroom. She would be a Waywayanda Artisan. She would be paid nothing. Every day she would drive in her black Toronado to a big horse barn and weave blankets.

Crystal made her announcement wearing her down jacket. The black Toronado was idling outside in the driveway. She pulled on her mittens.

"She's always been a manageable child," Mrs. Purty said to Mr. as if Crystal was not standing there. "She's always chosen the practical thing, once it was pointed out to her. I think she needs a relationship. People do funny things when they're looking for a man. Sylvia Gebhart took belly dancing. People try to run away from what they are, until they find they can't. Then they come home, when they can't make it out there on their own, and apologize to those they've hurt the most."

Crystal's mother was always half-right. It was the half-wrong Crystal had to get away from. She couldn't sort it out anymore. She had to get away from her mother's voice, the voice that hung there in the Purty house from morning to night like the living room curtains. She backed out of the driveway with a screech.

For ten years, Crystal had listened. She had tried to please her mother by becoming better-looking. She had bought all the magazines, applied all the creams in all the colors, rolled the hair rollers in all the directions. No matter what she did, she had the same shy, speckled eyes and flat lips. Even when her mother treated her to a complete make-over at the mall— to give her definition—nothing happened in the romance department.

The only person who had shown any interest in Crystal was

Tony De Santis, who serviced the black Toronado. Mrs. Purty was prejudiced against Italians, so Crystal respectfully limited her contact—she saw Tony only at six- and twelve-thousand-mile checkups. Just being in the Toronado was sometimes like being with him—he had a thing for her car and gave it a lot of extra care.

Crystal drove fast and well. Once she got past the stop-and-go traffic on the commercial part of Route 23, she got the Toronado up to eighty and kept it there. Superstitiously, she took the same route to Waywayanda that she had taken the first time. She and her friend Edie had found the Artisans by mistake on their way to New Paltz, New York, a few months before, in January. The Toronado had stalled—it was due for a tune-up—on a country road in front of a great pale weathered barn.

Crystal slogged through the mud in her high heels. A scattering of dull-colored, old-model Volvos and Saabs nursed at the barn's stone foundation. Inside, the darkness disoriented her. Strange piano music was playing. There were small tapping and clinking noises. A man and a woman were conversing in whispers. Crystal appeared to be alone with them.

"Excuse me," she said. The man's shiny black shoulder-length hair was held off his face with a headband like an American Indian's. The woman had long blond Peter Paul and Mary bangs. Crystal was shocked at her shapeless dress and ugly workboots.

"Can I help?" the woman asked.

"My car stalled." Crystal's voice came out a whine.

"It's yours, David," the woman said and strode silently away in the ugly boots. David held the barn door open for Crystal with one strong arm.

"Hey, nice!" he said, admiring the Toronado. His voice was gravelly and crude, urban, like Tony's. This was no American Indian—this was a Jersey Italian, a future version. For the next few hours, David had numerous men take a look at the Toronado. Unlike real mechanics, they lavished their time on experiments, improving things that weren't broken yet in the effort to find out what was. They were very genial; they told Crystal what it was like to be a Waywayanda Artisan. Crystal stood about the driveway, feeling very Jersey with her tight jeans, Montclair shoulder bag, and flipped hair—very excited to have so many men in and around her car.

When she got chilled, she wandered around in the soft, dark barn, occasionally checking on Edie, who sat shivering by the woodburning stove. What amazed Crystal most was that although the barn was a filthy mess, people were able to accomplish many difficult tasks. In each of the former horse stalls, there was a different activity—jewelry, pottery, woodworking, bookbinding, stained glass, silk screening, enameling, quilting. The women wore baggy dresses and had big clouds of kinky hair. They had innocent, preoccupied expressions as they worked.

The second story of the barn was a great, dim, raftered loft, reached by climbing a narrow ladder. It was awkward for Crystal to get to the top in her high heels, but what she saw there entranced her. Against the wall was a row of wooden looms with bright, hairy weavings creeping up their warps. Something began to stir in Crystal. She could almost feel the texture of the yarn between her fingertips. As she climbed back down the ladder, she ripped a little L in her blouse on a protruding nail, and to her surprise she wasn't at all sorry.

The Toronado was ready to roll. It now ran fine, though no one was quite sure why. Crystal reached into her shoulder bag for her navy blue checkbook, but David would not take one cent. As she watched the Artisans striding away together like a gang of cowboys, she wished that she could be around them all day instead of the mortgaged, married commuters at Azcom.

All the way to New Paltz, Crystal felt a quiet rise of color within herself. When the Artisans' catalog arrived a few weeks later, she could not get past the pages of finished blankets. She wanted to weave! It was the first time the still, small voice inside herself had said anything.

"Man has been a weaver since the Stone Age," Leelee said as she supervised Crystal wrapping the warp. "If your progress seems slow, think about his." Leelee was the woman with the Peter Paul and Mary bangs. She was tall and willowy, cold and beautiful. The other Artisan women were jealous. All the possible reasons Leelee confided tonelessly to Crystal as they sat side by side at the looms.

The Meads, who had started the Artisans, had discovered Leelee in Santa Fe on one of their trips west. Leelee had spent two years apprenticing herself to Navaho weavers. The Meads talked her into coming back to New York to take over the looms. The two women whom Leelee replaced had been learning weaving from a book. Angrily, they started a batik group.

Also, the Meads had appointed Leelee to the cabinet, the twelve policymaking Artisans, after only two months, whereas it took most people a year.

Then there was David. Everyone wanted to get close to David. He was admired as the master builder around the barn. He had saved the original rafters by engineering a complicated set of braces for the supporting beams. He had designed the office windows to frame the aspen grove outside. He had shored up the south half of the barn so the floor would be on the same level as the north half.

But he was aloof. He wasn't fun-loving or social like the other Artisan men. His private life was one of suffering. His wife was in and out of mental institutions. Right now she was in. She came up to the barn on Sundays to visit. Everyone thought he should stop wasting himself and get a divorce, but he felt bound to her. The only person he talked to about it was Leelee.

Leelee's spine listed toward Crystal's whenever she told her

David stories. Crystal swallowed them whole, even the complicated one about David and Leelee meeting secretly whenever they could in the shed out behind the barn. Crystal had never met people with problems like this, or if she had, her mother had kept it a secret.

David had Crystal's deepest sympathy. When she ran into him around the barn, he was always either building something or standing there like *David*, his weight on one leg, a hammer loosely hanging from one hand, his whole body at ease around a princely set of pectorals. Although Crystal gave him a rich hello, he never seemed quite sure, from meeting to meeting, who she was. He knew her in the Toronado and that was all. She wanted to help but was powerless to do anything, it seemed, but weave—and so she wove for David.

The weaving went slowly. Crystal worked for weeks and weeks before the first row of wool got wound on the shuttle and passed through the warp. Unlike the other novice weavers, she was not discouraged. She pleased Leelee—she was a quick learner, and she put in her nine hours a day on the cushion without complaint. Leelee rewarded her with secrets.

The other Artisans seemed to keep their distance. At the Meads' house, a rambling Victorian in the village of Waywayanda, Crystal was assigned the chilly basement room. No one gravitated down to visit. When she came upstairs, she had to do things the Waywayanda way, which made her feel awkward. All the residents helped cook, set the table, and clean up. After dinner, they sat around discussing philosophies and sharing adventures they'd had in other states. It was quite a change from Crystal's home, where her mother did everything, including all the talking.

Crystal's tight jeans hung in the closet unworn while she picked through the "help yourself" box at the barn for denim midis and army/navy jackets. She began to part her unflipped hair in the middle like Leelee. The day she got fitted for her first pair of workboots, she could almost hear her mother's pretirade groan echoing through the village dry goods store.

The only thing she kept from her other life was the Toronado. She loved knowing the roads from the village to the barn by heart, taking the corners fast, slowing down for the bumps, nosing the black beauty effortlessly into the sky at the top of the hill where the whole valley lay spread before her. Whenever she gave rides, she made all the Artisans kick the mud off their shoes first. She didn't care if they thought she was fussy.

On Sundays, when Joan came, Crystal used the Toronado to think in. Joan was David's wife. She had a round, sweet face, asymmetrical like a Picasso plate. She would sit at the piano in the barn office in a rose-colored dress, playing low, ponderous chords over and over beneath an unresolved melody. Leelee would get in a snit upstairs, intoning, "She's terrible for him—he's upset for two days before she comes and two days after she's gone." Crystal would break a warp thread, which took three hours to fix.

At lunchtime, David would guide Joan around the barn by the elbow as though she was senile; Joan would follow her hands, which she held in front of her like a plow. After that, she would need somewhere to lie down, and David would go away with her and not come back. Crystal would head for the Toronado. She would promise herself she would figure out—before Monday—what was wrong with what was going on. But on Monday she would be sitting before her loom again, side by side with Leelee, winding wool, absorbing secrets, weaving for David.

"This is rabbit brush," Leelee explained. It was June—Leelee was showing Crystal her dye garden. "The Navaho used it to make yellow. Depending on how mature the flowers were when they were boiled, the women could make anything from a bright canary yellow to a kind of olive green."

Crystal stroked the stubby plant respectfully.

"We almost got caught in the shed last night," Leelee continued in her low voice. "I'd like to kill the person who decided to start storing things there. Could we use your room tonight?"

The question came fast, and although it was a perfectly natural favor to ask, the answer was no. Crystal looked into Leelee's willful eyes and said, "Sure." A hundred and forty-four rows of indigo lay tightly strung in Crystal's loom. She was getting ready for the red. She couldn't wait to see the red stripe jump out against the indigo field. It was that which she concentrated on when she left the dye garden and climbed back up the ladder to the weaving loft behind Leelee, a greasy layer of jealousy in her stomach.

As the basement hideaway became a habitual meeting place for David and Leelee, things got better and worse for Crystal. Things got better because David gratefully made a point of befriending her. He took her on errands with him in his pickup truck, to the lumberyard, to the dump, to the building permit office next to the Demarest Cafe, where afterward he bought her an order of french fries. He never talked about himself, his life, his problems. He never mentioned Leelee. He just tried to be kind. When he called Crystal CP, the speckles in her shy eyes got dark and her flat lips got full. She'd never had a nickname before.

Things got worse because Crystal had nowhere to go at night. She stayed in the kitchen until eleven or twelve, talking to Michael Speck, a red-bearded beekeeper from Georgia who lived in the A-frame behind the Meads' house and did stained glass. Michael had a wild, peculiar laugh. He wanted to know everything there was to know about computer programming, and Crystal told him. When she heard the outdoors cellar door open and shut, she would go down to sleep in the smell of David and Leelee. She wanted to rant and rave like her mother would have: "Don't you two have any decency? Don't you even clean up after yourselves?"

In July the potters, Jerry Rasmussen and Dina Oboyek, decided to marry each other. They didn't want to wait too long, so they set their wedding day for the end of the month. Crystal was just preparing to weave her second red stripe into the indigo blanket, and she found the news distracting. The whole of the Artisans' attention went into the wedding preparations. David was building a gazebo in the Meads' garden where the couple were to take their vows. The jewelers were casting molds for silver rings. The quilters were proudly stitching away on a trapunto-bodiced gown—to their knowledge one had never been done. When David was asked to be best man, Leelee began to lobby with Dina to be maid of honor. She promised a blanket made by a very great Navaho weaver as a wedding present. The blanket was woven in diamond twill, a stitch so tight the Navaho could use the blanket to carry water all day, according to Leelee. There were very few weavers still living who knew diamond twill and would teach it—Leelee had the name of one in Ganado, Arizona. Dina was humbled by the gift.

A vegetarian reception was planned. Crystal, who still did not know any vegetarian recipes, was put on the cookie committee. Alone in the kitchen at night with Michael, she resentfully made six batches of her mother's coconut macaroons. Whenever she saw the radiant Dina being consulted about the festivities, she felt queasy with jealousy. She lay in David's smell at night, gouging her arms and wondering why in God's world everybody had somebody but her.

The night before the wedding, Crystal did not hear the cellar door open or close at eleven, twelve, one, or two. She fell asleep in her clothes on the daybed on the screened-in porch. In the morning, she was awakened by weeping. With a stiff back and a crick in her neck, she stumbled into the kitchen to see if the wedding had been called off. All the chairs and stools were occupied by women caught up in a common bittersweet silence. Leelee stood, impressively dry-eyed, at the center of attention, while Dina provided the sobs.

"I knew something was wrong," Leelee addressed the women in her confiding monotone.

"David and Leelee have been seeing each other," someone whispered to Crystal. "But now it's over. Joan got out."

"For the past few weeks," Leelee went on, "I kept asking him if something was wrong. He kept saying no, nothing was wrong. He knew she was getting out. All that time he knew. But he just couldn't bring himself to tell me."

This wasn't true. Leelee had told Crystal she'd gotten David to go for the divorce after all. Leelee had never been more sure of him. Crystal pressed her spine against the doorjamb to straighten it out. Leelee looked past her as if she wasn't there.

The garden was too bright—too red, too orange. Dressed to the hilt, the Rasmussen and Oboyek relatives formed their own little enclave on metal folding chairs in front of the gazebo. This was not their idea of a wedding. There wasn't even a minister. Sixty Artisans sat or lay about the grass and one of them now was Joan, looking legendary in a high-collared pink Victorian dress. Pain gnawed like a rat in her eyes.

David and Leelee were equally stone-faced beside the bride and groom. The air was tense and sultry and the bride was very hot. No one could hear her pledge. Tears poured down Crystal's face as she stood on tiptoe by the roses, watching the marital kiss.

In the shade by the porch, two girls in long calico dresses fanned flies off a fifteen-foot-long table laden with homemade breads, salads, rice, cookies, punch, and pies. The band, late in arriving, stood respectfully in the driveway with their instruments, smoking cigarettes and waiting for the ceremony to end. It was too warm to eat heartily, but people filled their plates anyway and stood in the yard talking about exactly what they would have been talking about if they weren't at a wedding.

David waltzed sadly with his wife—her hands looked perfectly normal disguised in his. Leelee was stationed amid her many new partisans; once in a while, her eyes would dart spasmodically toward the dancers.

Crystal stood alone by the Norway pine drinking punch. She watched Michael Speck lurching about the lawn drunk, scaring the Rasmussens and Oboyeks with his Georgia laugh. She knew he would ask her to dance if she hung around the band.

She wandered down the driveway instead, down the street to the black Toronado. She lounged in the passenger seat with the door open and the radio on. The local deejay was on an Eagles kick—he played one after the other. Crystal let her head fall back against the seat. She let the men sing to her about love found along the highway, heartaches, lying eyes. She wondered if the Eagles would like her or look right through her as if she wasn't there. She wondered if the Artisans really knew what they were doing. She decided to learn diamond twill. She would finish the blanket on her loom at the barn; then she would drive to Ganado. It would be strange to be alone again in a new place, telling people she met about this place. But she would feel at home, once she got behind a loom. She would be happy, sitting from early morning to late at night, weaving for David.

Baby Wood

The way Miss Willie was staring at my teeth was making me nervous. She was standing there, mean and skinny, the brim of her white sailor hat turned down as always to cover every strand of red, staring at me with her chin. She did everything with her chin—she sauntered around camp chin first like an Irish hoodlum. The other counselors may have been bossy, they may have been strict (and they were definitely fat), but they weren't wild like Miss Willie. Of course, they were Iowans; Miss Willie was from Arkansas. Was she going to hit me? There was a rumor that she had knocked a camper's teeth out for calling her Red. She hated her bright red hair. Rose and I had not called her Red, but we *had* pushed cross-eyed Trudy past the white birch fence, the dividing line between intermediates and seniors. The seniors had exercised their license to torture trespassers. They had caught Trudy, painted her face with clown paint, made her clean the fireplace in their lodge with a toothbrush.

I was afraid Miss Willie had sent Rose out of the cabin and ordered me to remain because she knew it was my idea. I saw her hand coming at me and I ducked. "Whoa!" she said, resting the hand on my shoulder. "I'm not going to hurt you." Her sergeant voice changed to a priest voice. "I'm disappointed in you. Something tells me this wasn't your idea. But that's no excuse. I want to know why you did it. Why?"

The tenderness in her voice was undeserved. If I dared swallow, I would cry. To keep my mind distracted, I concentrated on the objects on her nightstand, her rosary beads, her ukulele, the oval photograph of her mother, who looked like the bank president at home in Anamosa.

I didn't know why. All I knew was that Rose had quit lifesaving in the middle of the breaststroke requirement. She claimed she didn't care about badges anymore. We had always done everything together. Rose detested Trudy. Tricking Trudy seemed like something we could still do together.

"Look," Miss Willie said. "This kind of behavior should get

you and your friend two weeks of fire duty. I'll make it one week. But don't you miss one day, or you'll be gathering wood for the rest of the summer, so help me God." I wish she had slugged me, tied me up and burned my eyebrows off, done anything but be lenient. Now that I had disappointed her, tortured Trudy, and enslaved Rose, who hated fire duty, it was clear who the meanest person in camp really was.

Rose was lounging on a stump, clapping her thighs slowly open and shut, listing for me the beauty products she planned to buy at the drugstore when we got home to Anamosa. Her yellow hair fell over half her face. She had her log all picked out, and she had a decent-size stack of number 3 wood—sticks the width of three fingers stuck together. After half a week of fire duty, we knew the forest floor by heart, and this worked in her favor, not mine. I had given her the easy job and put myself in charge of baby wood. All Wo-He-Lo fires were started with a mound of baby wood, the finest, driest twigs, the scarcest in the forest. I had gathered the visible stuff the first day. Now I was scraping around under bushes with irritating sticky-backed leaves, coming up with nothing. The flies were biting and the gnats were rising like clouds of steam into my face every time I lifted a branch.

"Do you need help, René?" Rose asked.

"No."

"Just do number 1 wood and number 2 wood. She'll never know."

"Yes, she will!" I was surprised at the strength of my voice. It was almost like I was on Miss Willie's side instead of ours. "The fire won't stay lit on the first match. She'll know there's no baby wood."

"René, is something wrong with you?" Rose asked smugly. "You're no fun this year."

My whole head burned red. I hid it from Rose and began gouging up handfuls of dirt, pretending I'd found the twigs I wanted. "When I do a job, I do it right," I said. Until I turned around and saw her smirking at me, I fully believed this statement would inspire her.

"To each his own," she said. Where'd she get that phrase? Certainly not from me. She stood up and kicked her log down the path to the clearing where Miss Willie was fixing lunch. I could hear the wonderfully voluptuous scooping of Miss Willie's big spoon against the sides of her stainless steel bowl as she mixed biscuit dough. The hot dogs were no doubt already piled high, the Kool-Aid cooling. I was standing there with two handfuls of dirt, but I didn't feel sorry for myself—I felt sorry for Rose. She was losing her willpower or something like it. That would never happen to me.

I didn't like waking up at camp in the middle of the night. Three nights in a row I'd had bad dreams. I sat up on my cot. The light of the moon made the path outside our tent look like skin, lumpy and soft, marked with pocks. The trees looked like hair shafts magnified forty thousand times. In the morning, I would have to tread water. No one had ever really sat down with me and taught me how to tread water. I would have to jump in the pool and make up a way to do it.

At lunch, Rose had broken her word to me about the Pony and the Duck, two dirty-minded girls from Des Moines whom we had agreed to hate. The Duck had the first ducktail Rose and I had ever seen. The way the hair swept up in back seemed to me vaguely obscene. The Duck was always stripping to her big pointy Maidenform bra and pacing her tent, talking about Roy. The Pony, who had a long peroxide ponytail, had had a boyfriend for so long that she didn't have to talk about it. They weren't Wo-He-Lo types at all, yet their parents had signed them up for both sessions.

They had made fun of my doggie-in-a-blanket, which seemed especially unfair since they had both ruined theirs, holding the skewer in the fire so long that the biscuit blanket fell off, black as soot, into the flames. I had cooked mine to perfection, the dough crispy and golden all around, shrinking just enough so the red wiener tip could poke out. "Look at René's," the Duck had whispered.

"Oooooooh, what's his name?" the Pony had shrieked. Rose should not have laughed so hard or so long.

I sat on my cot, getting more wide-awake by the minute; I needed to use the woods. As I stepped out onto the steep path, I could see the moonlight edging up the hairy wall of Miss Willie's log cabin. It pressed through the screen and fell across the middle of her bed. The blanket looked tight and flat, as if no one was there. Now I would never get back to sleep.

"Rose," I whispered, climbing back under the sheets. I reached over to shake her and got a handful of hair.

"Mother?" She stirred a little.

"Rose, wake up," I said. "How do you tread water?"

"I'm putting ruffles on the little pumpkins," she murmured. She rolled over and pulled the pillow on top of her head. It bothered me that Rose had such lovely dreams. In my dream, I'd been caught with wet underwear in the stall of the girls' bathroom at school by a very mixed crowd—dozens of cousins, a few people from church, and Jack Webb.

The sky was very blue, very clear except for one dog-shaped cloud, drifting on its side from east to west. I was alone in the deep end of the swimming pool, not quite drowning as I tried to fulfill the three-minute treading-water requirement. With my bathing cap covering my ears, my gasping sounded so loud I scared myself. Every time my chin slipped below the water, my swallows sounded fatal. I was doing everything I could think of to keep afloat, flailing my arms, flapping my feet, forcing my legs to do the Mexican hat dance underwater.

Miss Willie was reclining above me on the diving board in her sailor hat, pointing her chin at the meadow, where I imagined she could see the seniors practicing their archery. We never thought of her as having such a beautiful figure until she put on her blue tank suit. Her dark glasses seemed to contradict the gold cross at her throat. At the sound of my sputtering and choking, she would check the stopwatch at her elbow and point her chin back at the meadow. I tried to cheat by holding my breath and sinking under to rest my muscles, but I was too winded to make it last. I was just developing a semieffective rotary shoulder move when she held up the watch—it had stopped—and yawned.

I stretched out on my back in a heavenly float. My calves were shuddering; my neck felt like it was stuck looking up. Miss Willie went sauntering down to the shallow end to tease her buddy, Miss Jo. I could see Rose and the Pony and the Duck in a huddle by the pool ladder, talking and fixing each other's straps. It was a hot, sunny day, but I couldn't feel the heat. I stood there at the side of the pool, waiting for the shower whistle, so cold I didn't think I would ever get warm.

Our three-day camping trip was foiled by rain. I was glad— Miss Willie was supposed to lose her temper easily in national parks. The tents in our unit were the oldest in camp; they leaked from every side. No one could sleep. Miss Willie invited us all to bring our sleeping bags down to her cabin. I felt safe there on her floor with twenty other girls. I wasn't afraid of my dreams. I slept well. In the morning, when it was still pouring, Miss Willie tried to get rid of us for a few hours by putting us on the juniors' crafts schedule. She sent us to the rock-polishing building. We rebelled—we pushed the little kids out of the way, turned the machines on high, and got ourselves kicked out. Outside the dining room, waiting for lunch, we had a mud fight. We stole extra desserts (even the seniors were envious of our rampage) and tramped back loud and wet to Miss Willie's cabin. We turned on the Duck's radio and listened to rock and roll from Cedar Rapids while we played gin rummy. Miss Willie paced around from screen to screen like in the movies when the heroine is waiting for word from the front. Finally she threw on her big yellow poncho, pulled her sailor hat down over her eyes, and slipped something secret into her pocket—the Pony said it was cigarettes. She went out right in the middle of lightning.

There was so much static that we turned the radio off and the Duck told us how she met Roy. She said she followed the advice of a magazine article, "Seven Secret Steps to the Man of Your Dreams." She took a long time to describe the process, which was basically two steps, not seven: she had to count a certain number of Oldsmobile 98 convertibles (her favorite car), and she had to keep silent for a certain number of hours and minutes (based on her month and day of birth). The first man she saw once she could speak again was Roy—the Man of Her Dreams.

I didn't believe a word of this because the Pony had told us earlier that Roy delivered the Duck's evening newspaper. Rose must have forgotten that. She seemed completely dreamy-eyed when the Duck described their first kiss. I could have been dreamy-eyed if I was somewhere else—lying down in a dark city apartment wearing a pair of beautiful new loafers. But kissing talk was not right at camp. For fifty years our founder, Miss Dot, had reminded us and our mothers before us and their mothers before them that Wo-He-Lo meant Work, Health, and Love—love for all mankind, not the individual.

By late afternoon, the rain had turned to mist. Miss Willie called us out of the cabin—she was just coming up the path—in time to see a fragile quarter arc of rainbow hanging in the clearing. We applauded.

It was still tremendously light in the west at bedtime. The sound of taps played by Miss Bev only made us feel more wide-awake. The wind was romantic; the crickets were trilling their fullest midsummer chorus; the whispering of girls was everywhere. I offered to tell Rose and Trudy a scary story, but Rose wanted to visit the Pony and the Duck. She sneaked out of our tent, then came back for me. "Come on!" she cried. "Everyone's out!" It was true. Girls in floaty nighties, girls in pastel pajamas were drifting down the dark paths to the porch of the cabin for one wonderful reason: Miss Willie was singing. Her sailor hat was pulled even further down over her eyes, but there she was, tapping a big white bare foot against the wood plank, strumming her ukulele.

"Tura-lura-lura," she sang. "When Irish Eyes Are Smiling." "Cockles and Mussels, Alive, Alive-O." Her voice was husky and lush, her pitch perfect. She slowed down the tunes in her own way, stretching her voice to cover the chords so that every song, no matter how cheery, was filled with longing. Some of us sang harmony on the choruses. My heart was bursting.

Night fell so slowly that even when it was finally pitch black, I knew which shadows were trees and which were tents, which of the silky dark hollows were paths and which were just my imagination. When someone snored, Miss Willie shifted the chords of her song directly into "Good Night, Ladies." We laughed and stood and stretched and sang that silly chorus all the way up the paths to our cots. Rose actually linked her arm with mine and we climbed with matched strides, knees bobbing in time.

At four in the morning, when I woke up, the moon was pouring down on our unit, bright as a kitchen light. The tents were the color of milk. I could see straight through the screens of Miss Willie's cabin to the white woods on the other side. Everything inside the cabin was smooth and flat—the walls, the floor, the bed. Miss Willie was gone.

Trudy was the only one in the tent the next day after swimming. I lay down on my cot to rest. I told her I'd done the fifty-five laps of crawl—I was getting the badge. She congratulated me. I didn't feel a sense of satisfaction so much as a sense of order. There was a lot of giggling and shrieking coming from the Pony and the Duck's tent. After listening to it for five or ten minutes, I sat up and looked across. A blond woman was sitting on the Duck's cot in a sea of yellow fur. The fur was Rose's hair and the woman was Rose with a ducktail. The Duck had the scissors. "Like it?" the Pony yelled.

"Believe me, she doesn't," Rose said. I couldn't answer. I couldn't look at her. She had been growing that hair since third grade. Every year we'd measured it together. Now it was littering the blanket and the floor—the Duck was flicking whole handfuls of it onto the dirt so she could fit her fat butt on the cot. I let them all go down to lunch without me.

There were three weeks of camp left after that, but I have no memory of them, except for Miss Willie's Elvis impression. She brought the house down on talent night, coming out on stage in the Drama Barn in white bucks, her red hair slicked back in a big pompadour, her ukulele on her thigh. "You ain't nothin' but a houn' dog," she sang, just like him, "just rockin' all the time." Our unit was particularly proud and we led the applause, but we found ourselves strangely outhooted by the counselors, who shamelessly went wild—Miss Jo was weeping. They stormed Miss Willie before she could finish her song.

I had been in the seventh grade for two weeks—long enough to consider myself an authentic junior high school student—when I received a purple mimeographed letter from Miss Fay informing all campers that there had been an accident. Miss Dot had had a heart attack while driving the Wo-He-Lo station wagon. The wagon had plowed into the propane tanks behind the dining room, blowing up it and Miss Dot. A fire had followed, a serious fire; a number of buildings had been lost and others damaged before the Boone Volunteer Fire Department had been able to bring the blaze under control.

I thought about the fire often. In my imagination it progressed rapidly through the dining room, ate its way neatly across the lawn where we had flag raising, then split into two sections. One burned through the junior cabins, then died out at the stand of rocks. The other section hit the Drama Barn. Devouring the smelly, dusty costumes and the rickety sets—everything was fifty years old—the fire got so vicious that it jumped the creek, whipped through the rock-polishing building, and swallowed the infirmary with a series of interesting miniature medicine explosions. It raged through the senior lodge in a matter of seconds and then, like a prairie fire, roared over the meadow to our unit and burned every one of our tents to the ground.

All that was left in my imagination was Miss Willie's log cabin, although sometimes two unrelated images would also pop into my mind: Miss Willie's empty bed in the moonlight and the shine of Rose's yellow hair in the blue silk pocket of my suitcase. I had saved as many handfuls as I could while they were all down at lunch—cross-eyed Trudy saw me—hoping that Rose would regret her decision once we got home and would be forever grateful to me for giving her back her hair.

Mr. Feathers

M showed up for work on Monday, May 19, with a striped suitcase and no engagement ring. She never told Mr. Reich what
her aunt and uncle said to make her leave. She never asked for
his help in finding a place to live. She just said she would be
available now, on nights when he wanted her to work late. He
didn't ask for an explanation.

They worked opposite each other at a large square walnut
table in his cluttered Chelsea apartment. Mr. Reich prepared
catalogs for German-made photoelectric equipment. He wrote
the German version and M translated his German into English.
Mr. Reich did not refer to whatever it was that had happened
to M, except by brewing their tea in his prized Meissen teapot
and spreading her melba toast extra thick with liverwurst.

After work, M walked east with her striped suitcase. She
stopped in front of the Dogwood, an old residence hotel off
Gramercy Park. She liked the picturesque, dilapidated façade.
She liked the way time did not seem to pass in the lobby. The
magazines were all a year out of date. Old people in the hotel
tearoom sat in floral chairs, digesting their meals.

M looked at room 19 on the second floor. It was dark. The
window facing the courtyard was covered with curtains of a
heavy, nostalgic material—dusty brown with big pink morning
glories climbing assertively up on the diagonal. The mirror of
the bureau was loose; it tilted forward, embracing the floor at
an awkward angle. The bed was a large, creaky Sears Roebuck
model, faced with mahogany veneer; M could see harsh white
sheets under the chenille spread. She sat down on the bed
in the dark and listened to the noises in the courtyard and
smelled the smells in the walls. When she was satisfied that she
could live there, she flipped open the two loud brass locks of
her striped suitcase.

M had loved ballet. She had worked hard in ballet school,
harder than the rest. But she looked foolish in a leotard. Her
shoulders were wide and her hips were wide. In the mirror

at the bar, she looked robust. When she saw this would never change, she quit. She wanted to spend her days doing something sterile. She met Mr. Reich. She translated German into English. She wasn't beautiful, but her nose was beautiful—long, with flaring nostrils and many interesting planes. Her black eyes were set wide apart. One seemed to say no, the other maybe. Sometimes she would feel repelled by the people around her; at other times she would surprise them by showing her deepest feelings. People always wanted an explanation for this. Mr. Reich was the only person who never wanted an explanation.

A man wanted to marry M. Her parents liked him, but on August 8, 1979, they were killed in a plane crash in Tenerife. Officials did not recover their bodies. Looking at the color photos of the rubble in *Time* and, from a different angle, in *Newsweek*, M thought she could see a scrap of her mother's coral paisley dress beside the burning plane. For weeks she could not translate German into English. Both her eyes said no.

The row house in Queens where M had lived for years went up for sale. Her aunt and uncle took her in. They arranged for the disposition of her parents' belongings. Her brother had the cherrywood sideboard shipped to Oregon with all the family silver still in the drawers. Other pieces went to friends or neighbors who were fixing up rec rooms or building additions. M took a pair of fine Swiss sewing shears. A yard sale was organized to get rid of the rest. It bothered M to see all the vases her mother had so hopefully filled with flowers sitting empty on a card table in the late afternoon light.

"All new," her fiancé told her. "Everything of ours will be new." He had many investment ideas. He wanted to go into business with M's uncle. At first they only wanted her share of the house proceeds. Then they wanted more. They took her to Johnny's 1890's. When the rolls came, they asked for the airline suit money too. It could have been that or something else which made her leave them all the next day.

M got through the week by working late. On weekends, she walked up and down Manhattan. The street scenes differed violently from neighborhood to neighborhood, but M did not prefer one scene to another. She just walked and looked. She could have been in a desert for all she cared or riding up and down an escalator in an airport.

Summer passed and M was pleased. She felt impermeable. Then the leaves began to turn. The red and yellow screamed life. M felt a wistfulness uncurl in her heart. Please, no, she would think as she walked. But she let the soft, aching thing uncurl.

On Saturday, September 20, at two-thirty it began to rain. M's black raincoat did not close properly. The rain splashed in and soaked the placket of her white blouse. She huddled in a glass bus shelter across from the Blackstone Cinema. People began to dribble out of the theater.

The last person to come out was a bald man in his early forties with wire-rimmed glasses. He stood under the marquee as if he had nowhere to go. He lit a cigarette and crossed the street to the bus shelter. The light reflected off his lenses so that M could not see his eyes. Except for that, he looked just like Mr. Feathers, her next-door neighbor when she was six.

Mr. Feathers was a teacher who grew tomatoes. He was always helpful to Mother and Father when the basement flooded or the car slid into a bank of snow. Every fall, when M skipped rope on her patio after school, Mr. Feathers stopped his raking to watch.

M felt a dangerous melting sensation in her chest. The bus shelter began to shimmer with possibility. The shape of Mr. Feathers' bald head made her feverish. The sight of his hand on his cigarette made her weak. It was a handsome, thick hand with short, neatly tapered fingers. Mr. Feathers brought the cigarette to his lips. The tip flared responsively when he drew in air. M was staring. She clung to the glass wall as if a blast of wind was pinning her there. Her white blouse was wet . . .

Mr. Feathers put the cigarette to his lips for the last drag and flicked it into the water at the curb. M listened to the sssst. "Want to get a cup of coffee?" He sounded as if he wasn't sure how to make the suggestion.

"Yes." Their bodies bumped awkwardly against each other as they moved out of the bus shelter into the drizzle. They took hands to steady themselves. At the corner Mr. Feathers hailed a taxi, which delivered them to the Hotel Dogwood. Never had the tearoom seemed so upbeat. "No names," M said.

"Okay." He folded his beautiful hands on the worn linen of the table. His wedding ring was plain and dull. Their coffee cups were empty.

Side by side they climbed the carpeted stairs to the second floor. M unlocked 19 and pulled back the top sheet of the bed. Mr. Feathers sat down on the sheet in his raincoat with his knees wide apart. M stepped between his legs and lifted off his glasses. He tipped his forehead toward her so they would come off gracefully.

He reached up to unbutton her blouse. The threads were swollen tightly around the buttons. Mr. Feathers was very patient. He spent a lot of time on each button. M loved the gentle, busy touch of his hands grazing her bare throat and her chest. He still had four buttons to go when he got his first good look. Her breasts were round and large with deeply colored areolas. Her nipples were crinkled and erect, shining like thimbles.

Mr. Feathers lost patience and pulled the blouse down as far as it would go, binding her arms and her wrists to her side. He closed his eyes while he stroked her breasts. M felt like she was flying. She could see his erection pushing against the inside of his slacks. He wrestled his way out of his raincoat and unbuckled his watch. He pulled his sweater over his head. His torso was smooth and hairless, his biceps nicely developed— from the neck down, he looked like a lifeguard. M watched his muscles flex as he reached under her red plaid skirt. He stroked her wide hips. Her eyes showed embarrassment. He spread her legs open with his knee and plunged both hands between. She flinched. He undid his fly. His cock flopped out through the zippered edges into his fist. He had himself in his left hand and her in his right. All he had to do to put them together was stand up. When he did, she cried out and wrapped her knees around his waist. Her head fell back. He braced her against the wall, her arms still confined in the blouse. She shivered when he kissed the soft underside of her throat on the pulse.

M opened one eye. The room was very dark. She was lying on her stomach. Her insides were ringing like the strings of a grand piano after a concert. Her fingers were plastered together. Her legs were sore. One corner of the sheet was wrapped around her waist. The rest trailed off the bed and onto the floor.

Mr. Feathers was gone. M listened to the night for some evidence of him. She felt a road had been opened in her heart that led out into the world and vanished in a woods. She began to sweat with fear. At the end, he had tried to change the no-names rule. She wondered if he had persuaded the desk clerk to tell him anything.

M wanted him back. She rose and took the silver shears from her suitcase. She walked to the heavy brown curtain and cut a slash in a pink morning glory. Then she snipped it out neatly around the edges, petals, leaf, and stem, leaving no pink on the brown and no brown on the pink.

For days afterward, M was unnerved. Pornographic images flashed uncontrollably in her brain, but never when she needed them. They flashed when she was in line at the drugstore or in the middle of a sentence with Mr. Reich. When she was alone, she tried to force the details into her mind, but they began to blur. Comic and mundane versions of Mr. Feathers' face replaced her memory of him.

M went looking for Mr. Feathers. She stood in the bus shelter across from the Blackstone Cinema. She looked for him in store windows, in telephone booths, in idling, double-parked cars. For weeks she stared, she squinted, she craned her neck. She begged people's pardon for knocking them aside to get a closer look at some bald head in a passing bus. The harder she looked, the more she lost her claim on him.

In October, Mr. Reich accepted a rush order from a Frankfurt manufacturer for a two hundred–page catalog. M was able to work every weekend. She drank too much coffee, slept poorly, and came down with a cold. She worked and worked, gulping cold pills, dragging herself out of bed. Mr. Reich heated soup for her supper and sent her home in a taxi.

On Halloween, at nine-thirty, she climbed the stairs to 19. She stopped on top of the landing to fumble in her pocket for a tissue. Her beautiful nose was running. Down the hall beside her door a man was standing, had been standing for hours, to judge from the way his head was bowed and his back seemed to be part of the wall. M's body temperature rose. Anxiety strangled her. She put her key in the lock without looking at him.

"I've been thinking," he said. The pitch of feeling in his voice disturbed her.

"Don't think." M sat down on the bed in her raincoat and turned on the lamp. She sneezed. He took off his glasses and folded them carefully. He sat down beside her.

"I need to call you something," he said. She told him about Mr. Feathers. She gave him her first initial. It hurt her to feel his hands on her buttons again.

He came every Monday and Thursday from five to seven. They developed a little routine that pleased them. M would lie naked on the bed with her arms stretched over her head. He would hold her down and stroke her breasts and thighs. His fingers moved intelligently over her body, reading it as if it was braille. She would wriggle and thrash against his restraining arm. She would get carried away and jump on top of him. He told her how much he liked to see her sliding all over him; he loved the looseness in the corners of her mouth. She kept her eyes closed until she reached a climax; then she opened them. She felt that a little piece of her was leaking through her irises onto his face.

Afterward they slept, sprawled like corpses or snuggling like children. M would rise first and shake him awake. He never wanted to leave. "Nothing and no one," she would answer flatly every time he asked her what she did on weekends and with whom. She noticed that he felt compelled to leave her dazed, depleted, and sore. She began to leave bite marks on his torso, so he would have to undress in the dark at home, wherever that was.

"It's psychosomatic," he said one afternoon when he was doubled over, waiting for a sudden, sharp chest pain to go away. It was a Wednesday, the day before Thanksgiving; he had managed to sneak in a visit.

"Does it happen often?" M asked.

"Only since I met you."

"Don't joke," M said. She helped him move slowly toward the bed. "Lie down."

When he could breathe freely, she began to arouse him again. He caught her hand in his. "Let's just hold each other today," he said. "There's never enough time to hold. If I could come three days a week, we could spend one whole evening just holding."

"Holding wouldn't be enough for me."

He wasn't listening. "We could get an apartment. We could furnish it together. We could eat afterward."

"Be quiet."

"I have other ideas," he said. "About weekends. Trips."

"They will never happen."

Mr. Feathers felt thwarted and restless. He let her fingers slip out of his hand. Her hand moved down his torso and she began to finish what she had started.

Their routine began to seem a bit rehearsed. The tormented look in his eyes began to seem a bit jaded. He made love with less exhaustion. He seemed to be able to come and go on time with no special agony. "Is everything okay?" M asked one afternoon.

"We need to get out of here," he said. "We need something new." M led him down the hall to the great white tub standing on four claws in the communal bathroom. She washed him and soaped him everywhere she could think of. He left with a look in his eyes that was truly unwise.

Mr. Reich had plans to spend Christmas in Frankfurt with his son. He would be able to hand-deliver the catalog copy. His flight was scheduled to leave at five in the morning on Monday, December 22.

M finished proofing the final draft at midnight the night before. She wished Mr. Reich a safe flight and kissed him goodbye. Back in her room, she lay awake for hours, brittle and jittery.

She was still dreaming when she heard a knock on the door. She threw back the sheet hysterically. She thought she was late for school. She thought she was home again.

"Merry Christmas!" Mr. Feathers said. He was happy as helium, holding a stack of shining presents, red and green boxes tied with black satin and gold rope, festooned with star-shaped bows. He pushed past her into the room and lowered the pile of gifts carefully onto the unmade bed. He handed one to M.

"Open it," he said.

M lifted the large square white cover of the florist's box back on its hinge. Lying inside on a taped green stem with a spray of fern was a dewy cream-colored gardenia, its fragrance heavy and sweet. M began to understand that he was going away. She felt like an orphan, a prisoner. "When are you leaving?" she asked sullenly.

"In a few hours," he admitted.

"And when are you coming back?"

"Ten days."

M threw the box on the floor and threw herself against the door. "Not ten."

"Everyone else is going for twelve," he said. "I'm coming back early—to be with you."

"Five," she begged.

He stared at the floor. "I can't."

"Six?" Her lips began to quiver and her voice deserted her. Laboriously, she whispered, "I can't wait ten." A look of hatred flitted over her face. She despised exposing herself. Did that mean she loved him?

"I'll try," he said. M felt perverse. She would have to make an honest man of him whether he liked it or not. She opened the presents in the order of smallest first. She got zebra barrettes, bubble bath, petits fours, an AM/FM radio, a book of colored floral engravings, pink jeans, and a silly black thing.

"Put it on," he said.

He looked for a classical station on the radio while M slipped out of her nightgown and into the silly black thing. Her nipples poked out of the holes in front. Stiff black ruffles rose over her hips and framed the lips of her exposed vagina. M stood sadly in front of the falling mirror. Static strains of "The Nutcracker Suite" emerged from the radio. M looked ridiculous.

Mr. Feathers was wild. "Dance!" he said.

"The Nutcracker" sounded laughable, cartoony. M felt clumsy and shy. "I can't," she said.

"Please?"

M executed a mock arabesque. Mr. Feathers couldn't tell it was mock. "More!" he said. She made a prissy face and moved across the room on her toes, cradling the air with her arms.

Mr. Feathers leaned against the bureau, unbuckling his belt and taking his cock in his hand.

M whisked a festive red sheet of tissue paper out of one of the boxes on the bed. As the violins plunked childishly away, she snapped the tissue at her side like a tango scarf. She snatched up a gold rope and danced over to the bureau, where Mr. Feathers was getting harder and redder.

"Hey, don't," he said as she tied his wrists together behind his back. M pirouetted to the bed. She whipped black satin ribbon into the air like a lariat. She danced up to him and tied each one of his ankles to the bureau legs.

"Ow!" he said. "Looser." But M kept the ribbon tight. She gathered up the self-adhering bows and stuck them all over Mr. Feathers. Then she stood on her tiptoes in first position and began to pull on her nipples. She dipped to a deep plié and, with her knees spread wide, stroked herself between the ruffles. As the full orchestra thundered, Mr. Feathers' erection waved in the air. M slipped on her raincoat and waved good-bye.

"Cunt!" he swore. He tore his hands out of the gold rope and bent over to untie his feet. He grabbed M as she unlocked the door and threw her down on the bed. Gripping her hips from behind, he hammered away between the ruffles. Sweat poured through his shirt and the bows fell off on the sheet. After he came, his erection did not disappear. His face was still intent. He grabbed M by the hair and hammered away inside her again and again.

Sunlight streamed in through the hole in the curtain. The room was littered with debris. M was asleep uncovered in bed. Mr. Feathers dressed carefully. He put on his overcoat, covered M, then sat down beside her. "I am a family man," he said to the wall. M's eyes flickered open. She stared into the pillow, so he wouldn't know. "I own a menswear shop in Westchester. Last year was my best year so far." He paused. "What else? I'm an Orioles fan. I own stock in a new calculator company. My kids are good kids. My name is Jack." He said it louder. "My name is Jack. Jack!" The syllable burned in M's ears.

She heard him rifling around in her suitcase—she was afraid for a minute that he was looking for things to remember her by, that he wasn't coming back. He crossed the room, opened the door, and pulled it shut again.

On Christmas Day, M ate boiled ham in the tearoom with the old people. Then she sat on her bed and ate petit fours one after another until they were all gone. In the middle of the night, she staggered out to the hall bathroom and threw up. In between heaves, she cried for her mother.

For five days, she told herself it was no good. It wasn't a life. Alone on every major holiday. Never able to share a pet. She wasn't real without his touch. Her neck and back felt stiff as cement. Her body seemed to angle away from her mind like the reflection of a knife in half a glass of water. She planned to end it with him. She felt better once this was decided. She went out for a walk. She walked up and down Manhattan. Manhattan was dead—she came back unrefreshed. She stared at the flower she'd cut out of the curtain; she wanted to hurt herself with the shears. She loved him.

On the sixth day—M pictured him tearing himself away from a band of ruddy, blond, brightly dressed, laughing skiers—she dressed in her white blouse and red plaid skirt and raincoat and sat on the bed. She listened all morning and all afternoon and long after nightfall she heard him. She heard Jack—his train was in the station, his taxi in the street, his footsteps in the hall.

Resident Artist

"Oh, I dabble, I dabble," Viola said. "But you must meet Eleanor. Eleanor is our resident artist."

I was applying a coat of white mat paint to the walls of the former town clerk's office in Dustin, New York. It was the summer of '68; the air was hot and still. I had the door open so the paint would dry faster. Viola nearly filled the doorway. Ever since she had found out I was opening an art gallery across the highway from her luncheonette, she had started wearing big arty jewelry over her sleeveless nylon tops.

"Eleanor did a sketch of a cherry tree in bloom which received a lot of attention in our adult education class," Viola said. Her voice was actually getting snooty. "You missed a spot." I rolled the roller back and forth over the bluish stain, but it bled through. "Given half a chance, Eleanor could be famous," Viola said arrogantly, almost blamefully. "With you in town, Tamara, it's very likely, wouldn't you say?"

"The art business is not that simple," I said with authority, though I was just guessing—it was all new to me. I would have to be more selective about the half-truths I told Viola. She had wanted to know what I was doing here; I had attributed to myself an ideal, a desire to promote little-known artists in a little-known setting, where art was needed most. I hadn't mentioned the married man connected to me at all times (in my mind at least) along Route 1, the back way to Wickley. Why else would a girl with long blond hair, a B.A., and six thousand dollars settle alone in the middle of nowhere?

"Well, is it possible?" Viola whined. She hung there in the doorway like a giant Kewpie doll, ready to be taken home by the first paying customer. My arm was tired. I cradled the roller in the paint tray.

"It's possible," I said.

Twice during the next couple of weeks, when I went into the luncheonette for a newspaper, I had just missed Eleanor. "She was just here," Viola would say. "I told her all about you. She wants to meet you."

"Good," I would say. "I'd like to meet her."

Most of the people who came to my first opening, a show of clay masks with Haida Indian motifs by a guy named Anton from New Jersey, came because they thought the gallery was the annex to the antique store next door. Viola was an exception. "Eleanor wanted to come too," she said. "But she's so busy with the farm. And the children—she's got the eight. I have to keep reminding her that art should come first."

"Good," I said. "It should."

We repeated ourselves a month later at my second opening, a show of wood and straw constructions by a sculptor from Woodstock. A few of my artist friends came at my request. Viola, the only local there, heard me offer them shows. "Oh, you should give Eleanor a show!" she cried.

"Viola," I said, careful to avoid a sarcastic tone, "I've never seen her sketches. I've never even seen *her.*"

Viola's face collapsed for a moment. Then she recovered. "I'll get that sketch to you," she said. "With or without Eleanor."

It was November—and cold—the day Viola left the luncheonette unattended long enough to run across Highway 6, throw open the gallery door, and shout, "Tamara, we're set! Saturday! Eleanor's free!"

Henry, the owner of the antique store, was in the gallery warming up with a cup of coffee. He had a knack for appearing soon after I had brewed fresh coffee, made myself a sandwich, or opened a box of doughnuts. I began to think he could smell food through the wall we shared, perhaps through the bluish stain. "Bet you I know why Eleanor's free," he said.

"Why?"

"It's hunting season. Her husband's hunting."

"So?"

"He don't like her to go nowheres unless he goes somewheres. He wants her car *in the driveway* when he gets there. You should see them sometimes, trying to beat each other home!" He laughed with glee, as if, being a bachelor, he was getting away with something: he never had to bother laying down the law to a woman. He was an innocent man, and yet what he described left a cold, clamping sensation in the pit of my stomach, the same sensation I felt when I saw my parents' life insurance policies side by side—Dad's life was worth sixty thousand, Mom's ten.

Early Saturday afternoon, Viola brought Eleanor to the gallery with her sketch. Eleanor wore a man's old khaki car coat over a man's plaid flannel shirt. She was on the tall side and too thin, her eyes deeply sunken in their sockets. "Show Tamara your garnet," Viola instructed.

"Oh!" Eleanor flashed a wide, spooky smile which seemed to me a dangerous waste of energy. She reached beneath her shirt and pulled out a thin gold heart on a chain. A garnet filled one curve of the heart. "It's different," Eleanor offered.

"It's beautiful," I said. "Did your husband give it to you?"

Viola howled—a lengthy physiological event, her bust and stomach clapping together in great wallops while she helplessly surveyed the ceiling.

"No, I don't think so," Eleanor said.

"I gave it to her," Viola said, wiping her eyes. "Last year."

"For my thirty-third birthday," Eleanor said. She looked fifty.

The sketch of the tree was done in pen and ink, mounted and framed by Eleanor with a wide powder blue mat. The whole thing was wrapped in saran. I held it at arms' length and looked at it for quite a while. Eleanor joined me. She seemed to marvel at her own work, the way a woman would marvel at her sleeping child. It was very, very good. Something sprightly in the technique gave the tree life. I told her so.

Eleanor responded with a long rehearsed description of which bough she had drawn first and which rock she had sat on to draw it and so on through the entire drawing. Her dentures clicked against the roof of her mouth as she talked. I told her to bring in the rest of her work. Her face came to a complete halt. "This is the only one she has matted," Viola explained.

"Don't worry about it," I said. "I don't need a mat to appreciate what I'm looking at." Eleanor seemed unrelieved. I offered them coffee. They hemmed and hawed and then, when they coaxed it out of me, I amended the offer to include white wine. We drank a whole bottle. Viola led a discussion, largely bitter, about men which ended when I told them what I looked for in a man. "Openness and honesty," I said. Eleanor looked at me as if I had said, "Three penises."

We closed by agreeing that we should all do this again soon, but from then on, whenever Eleanor's brown Chevy station wagon passed the gallery, it contained anywhere from five to nine silhouettes and was heading north, home, at full speed. Very often, a slow silver truck chugged by in its wake.

Viola began to talk about Eleanor's show as if it was already on the gallery calendar. I reminded her that I had still seen only one sketch.

The holidays came; I flew to L.A. to visit my older sister, Nora. She completely disapproved of me and my choices in life, but I had nowhere else to go for Christmas. I wasn't about to sit around in my room behind the gallery, waiting for a fast, hushed, unsatisfying phone call from Wickley while round after round of in-laws, family members, and friends filed through his wreath-covered door. It was nice at my sister's place. The beach was warm; the sky was blue. I kept postponing my return flight—I was gone a month. I almost sadistically enjoyed the disappointment, the anxiety in his long-distance voice each time he asked when I was coming back.

"Eleanor's never going to bring the rest of her sketches in," Viola greeted me my first day back in Dustin. "If you want to see them, you're going to have to go over there." We went together.

Eleanor lived in a ranch house that badly needed painting. The front stoop was a stack of cinder blocks. She met us at the door with a hollow light in her eyes. There were nine empty hooks on the living room wall with nine pairs of galoshes underneath. On the tenth hook was Eleanor's khaki car coat. The floor was covered with linoleum. Something smelled of manure. "This is my office," Eleanor said, sweeping us over to an old steel file cabinet which had been painted powder blue.

"Show Tamara the still life," Viola said.

Eleanor pulled out a drawer and thumbed through the files. "Let's see," she kept saying. "Still life. Still life." All she came up with was farm bills. She tried another drawer. I looked out the picture window. The metal mailbox, also painted powder blue, leaned away from the road on its post as if shrinking from contact. Eleanor disappeared from the living room. When she returned, she had a violin under her chin and was playing it. Viola and I eventually left.

In April, I put together a group show featuring landscapes in a variety of media by local artists. I included Eleanor's sketch. A reporter from the weekly brought a photographer out to the gallery to give me some prepublicity. I found myself pointing them toward the cherry tree. Eleanor's art was on the front page.

I hoped the exposure would launch her—in her own eyes at the very least. I called her to see how she felt about it. "Yegads," she kept saying, as if she was the center of a scandal.

On Sunday afternoon, about an hour before the opening was scheduled to begin, Eleanor parked her brown Chevy wagon across the highway, facing home. She was wearing an out-of-date two-piece suit, probably an Easter outfit. She looked uncomfortable in high heels. "Look around," I said as she entered, but she seemed intimidated by the expanse of polished oak floor. She pulled a folding chair up to the big display window by the door and sat with her eyes on the highway. I uncorked the wine, laid out the cheese and crackers. Henry came in from next door as if on cue.

"Congratulations!" he said to Eleanor. "You're famous!" She grimaced. He chewed a while. "Where's your husband at?"

"Down to Hapsburg." She cast her eyes south. "Looking at a used harvester."

There was a lull during which I simply stood across the

room from Eleanor watching her watch the road. Then everything happened at once. Cars rolled into Dustin and parked along both shoulders of the highway, constricting traffic to one lane. The phone started ringing with calls from people who were lost. I was giving directions to someone when I saw Eleanor climb up on the folding chair in her stocking feet. She cupped her hands to her eyes like blinders, leaning precariously against the glass. "Ye-gads!" she swore. That is my final memory of her. She clambered down in her Easter suit, awkward as a foal, stabbed both feet into her heels, and ran out the front door just as a swarm of guests tried to get in. *Walk*, I want to tell her whenever I remember her, *take your sweet time*. The silver truck was stuck so long in gallery traffic that before it was able to chug past the window, three different ladies had had time to scan the oils, acrylics, and watercolors and remark to me their special interest in the cherry tree.

Hooked

I had lived in the hamlet of Dustin only a week when the fire whistle went off; a louder, uglier blast would be difficult to imagine. I was driving somewhere in a big hurry, but I stopped to watch the engine roll out of the Dustin Hook & Ladder garage. Hale of Hale's Sunoco, next door, jumped on the running board as the engine swung north; other volunteer firemen around town commandeered trucks, station wagons, whatever was available to get to the fire. If wives and children were aboard, they went too; otherwise they stood around the crossroads speculating about what was burning and why. I was in a hurry, as I said, so I had to read about the fire in the local paper—the Lunds' barn was lost. I passed its charred foundation the next day on the way to do my grocery shopping. A woodworker I knew in Greeley called me up to complain. He had just given the Lunds a price to take the barn apart; he wanted to use the hand-hewn beams, all hemlock over a hundred years old, and the handsome weathered siding for renovations. He was outraged at the waste and so were the Lunds— the barn was uninsured.

The next week when the fire whistle went off, I was in a motel room forty-five minutes away, probably just starting to undress. The man who was the only reason why I was living in Minnisink County was married. Driving home on Route 1, I was dazed and depleted; my heart was raw. I zipped right past the smoking embers, the engine, the chaotic spray of familiar Dustin vehicles without any of it registering. Viola, my luncheonette buddy, told me that another beautiful old barn had been lost.

A month later, in late September, a state police car pulled into the driveway of the green house across the highway and took away Plain Glen. His partner in crime, who lived two miles up the highway, was in the back seat in handcuffs. Both men confessed to setting fire to twelve barns in the last two years, fires which they then helped put out in their capacities as volunteers; both were sent to Sing Sing. At first I was infuriated at the material loss. People I knew were actively looking for barns to live in; the supply was dwindling; the ones Plain Glen had destroyed were architecturally irreplaceable.

I had seen Plain Glen in person only a few times, on September evenings, standing out in his front yard smoking a cigarette. He kept his back to the house as if he was trying to put it all behind him. He was a slight man—the waist of his pants pouched in two places where his belt was drawn through. His face looked as if he'd been pulled from the womb before his features had fully developed. He smoked in that elaborate, compensatory way of people who are not very involved in their lives. When he inhaled, he concentrated as if for that interval he was employed, which Viola assured me he was not. It seemed a game with him to swallow as much smoke as possible. The butt he flicked away in a neat wide arc that ended just outside his front yard.

Plain Glen left a wife and five children behind in the green house, but people in Dustin felt sorry instead for his mother. "Poor Thea, it's breaking her heart," they said in the post office. I learned from Viola that Plain Glen's mother was big in the Dustin Presbyterian Church. The congregation counted on her for table decorations, which she produced for function after function using construction paper, glitter, and very little else. Glen's father, of course, was a highly respected major landowner like all the Ritchies before him. Plain Glen's arson could only have its source, people implied (though Viola begged to differ), in his wife, a tiny, squinty-eyed fireball of a woman, a divorcée from West Virginia.

I met his wife, Glorine, because she had nothing to do but get the mail. She drew out her expeditions to the post office so long, dropping in at Viola's luncheonette, at Henry's antique store, at my gallery, that it seemed the children back in the green house were raising themselves. I loved the rich, raunchy twang in her voice and she loved to talk. She told me things that were none of my business, though she was right in thinking (if she did think it out) that she could trust me. She started and ended each tale by singing, "I tell you!"

"I tell you!" she sang one day. "Sex with him was a one-way street. I felt just like a garbage disposal. I told him so, so I ain't telling you something he don't know. And do you know what he done when I told him? Instead of trying to correct the situation, he goes and disappears to Port Raccoon, tells his ma he's looking for work, and spends the weekend with a woman I know! I tell you!"

The day Glorine got the papers finalizing Plain Glen's sentence, an indeterminate term of three to five years, she ran over to the gallery to ask me what "indeterminate" meant. I told her. When she understood there was leeway there, she mobilized herself to take on the authorities. The warden had eaten the cake she had baked from scratch without a recipe and patiently towed to Ossining on visiting day. The warden claimed it was their policy. I had the feeling Glorine had planned to get back at him by seeing just how early she could get Plain Glen out. Based on the way he had stood in the front yard with his back to the green house, I wondered if he wanted out at all. He was building coffee tables in prison (Glorine was outraged that she couldn't have one); he had three square meals a day; for sex he had Mary Palmer and her five daughters—Glorine's Appalachian euphemism for masturbation. I thought it sounded like a good life for Plain Glen; I thought that even before I finally accepted Glorine's invitation to visit the green house.

It smelled of urine. Plain Glen's three-month-old twin boys lay in separate playpens in the living room watching "Let's Make a Deal." Glorine poured store-brand cola into a yellow Melmac coffee cup for me. Her daughters by her first husband avoided us; they passed through the kitchen once, made up with Glorine's lipstick and rouge, hugging the wall as if to escape a sudden blow. Her three-year-old, Glen Junior, did the opposite. He openly defied Glorine within striking range and remained there at her feet to take his blows. He was wailing from one such whack when Glorine's mother-in-law, Thea, popped her head through the back door. She dropped a bag of unripe pears from her tree onto the counter and swept up Glen Junior, cooing, "Uh-oh, did mean old Mommy hurt Grandma's little Princey-Wincey again?" She actually said that.

In response, Glen Junior gritted his teeth and pinched Thea's large, soft upper arms so hard his cheeks shuddered. She pried away his fingers and he started to kick. She held his knees still while continuing to kiss and coo. I believe she thought she was doing the Christian thing, turning the other cheek. She was there only a few minutes, but before she left she addressed Glen Junior exclusively on a wide range of topics—the stale air in the kitchen, the possible brain damage of his sisters, the high price of cigarette smoking. Glorine blew Pall Mall smoke out the door after her and dropped the pears in the garbage. She grabbed Glen Junior by the collar and yanked him into her lap.

"I tell you!" Glorine grinned. "See how she favors him. She don't even sneeze at the twins. She thinks they ain't Plain Glen's. That's why she makes me get by on welfare. She don't help at all. She don't know nothing! It's *him* ain't Plain Glen's"—Glen Junior beamed at me conspiratorially—"I was two months gone when we met. I tell you!"

An entire year in Dustin had gone by before I understood the creative aspect of what Plain Glen had done. I was packing my stuff after many weeks of strain and moving permanently to "our" apartment in Gardnerville. My married man hoped to join me soon, though he couldn't say when; he was having a torturous time trying to tell his wife and daughter about us. The situation was crippling my ability to feel any deliciousness, any escape during our trysts. I was sick of it, sick of the secret, sick of myself, sick of Dustin and all the people who were probing my reasons for leaving without letting on how much they already knew.

When the fire whistle went off, the ugly blast sounded almost nostalgic—we hadn't had a good fire around here since Plain Glen had been put away. I threw down my carton and ran out to the highway. The Dustin Hook & Ladder engine was just swinging east on Route 1, the usual motley fleet of volunteers in its wake. I jumped in my blue Saab to follow. Clouds of black smoke could be clearly seen over the next hill, but the roads to the property took us north and east before we could zigzag back.

The driver killed the siren as he turned into the driveway. The men uncoiled the hose and ran with it down to Dustin Pond. They had a pump—they hoped the pond held enough water. The family stood there watching in passive disbelief as their dairy barn was destroyed.

The blaze seduced one wall at a time, licking its way along the beams and floorboards, consuming wood, machinery, and straw with equal interest and appetite. The water came through, but too little, too late. The firemen had to content themselves with hosing down the side of a storage building, so it wouldn't catch. Fire poured up through the timbers, crashing against the sky, loud as Niagara Falls. For one magnificent moment, the structure was transparent. It shuddered briefly, then it toppled. The flames multiplied like rats, feeding, gorging on what remained. There were low voices, prayerful tones, as friends and neighbors offered tools and free labor to the family if they wanted to rebuild. One of the firemen was flirting with one of the wives, embarrassing her—she was dying to flirt back. There was rapture in the event. I wanted to drop Plain Glen an anonymous postcard saying I understood.

Red Spikes

Glorine and Viola were huddled over their morning coffee in the Dustin luncheonette, a yellow frame building at the crossroads of Route 1 and Highway 6. Viola's seashell collage lay to one side, a day late for the Minnisink County Fair competition. Viola's husband, Bud, was too busy to deliver the collage to the pavilion in Gardnerville, and Viola herself was stuck in the luncheonette without a car. "It was supposed to symbolize peace," she said with cultivated disgust. Viola was obese, but she still wore bright red pants, her trademark since the days when she was a local beauty queen.

Glorine tapped the burdened purple paper with authority. "Best damn symbol of peace *I've* seen!" she sang.

"Thank you!" Viola smiled gratefully. The leopard headband which held her long black hair off her face crept forward in the August heat.

"It's true," Glorine crooned. Since her husband, Plain Glen, had been sent to Sing Sing for arson, the stool by the cash register had become hers. Standing four-foot-ten in her red pigtails, Glorine would sooner be taken for a twelve-year-old than a woman with five children. "You're looking at ninety-two pounds of passion from the hills of West Virginia!" she would crow by way of introduction. People who lived in Dustin were suspicious of her because she had two daughters from a former marriage.

Glorine crumpled her week-old cigarette pack and left it on the counter. "I'd have to buy tobacco off the vine and dry it myself to get one smoke from my food stamps," she said cynically.

Viola extracted a new pack of Pall Malls from the dispenser behind her and put it beside Glorine's coffee cup. "Don't tell Bud," she said.

"I wasn't begging," Glorine said softly. "But thank you kindly just the same."

"You're entirely welcome."

Glorine pulled the cellophane off the package with ritualistic concentration. She offered Viola a cigarette and lit a match. Both women leaned complacently into the flame with half-closed eyes. The tips of their cigarettes glowed orange. Glorine shook out the match, smoke pouring out her nose in dragon gusts. Viola exhaled by extending her lower lip. The smoke went straight up, then over her shoulder. Both women turned to look out the window.

The glass was hazy with road dust except for two round, eye-level patches Viola had cleaned with Windex, one for herself and one for Glorine. She refused to maintain the luncheonette any more than that. She let the stools get torn, the walls get yellow, the black-and-white linoleum get worn down to the wood. Still people came in. Twice that morning she had had to cook bacon for strangers.

Outside, the red lights of the road work barricades flashed hypnotically on the uneventful landscape. For two weeks the county road crew had been replacing a culvert a quarter mile down where the railroad tracks crossed Route 1. "I'll be sorry when they're gone," Glorine said tenderly.

"Your mother-in-law won't," Viola said. "She was complaining about you again today. How you deprave yourself. Every afternoon. Standing out there in the road like a harlot, talking and laughing with five married men."

"She can't make one married man laugh, let alone five," Glorine said. "Besides, they miss me if I don't show. And I don't *do* nothing. She knows that."

"If it wasn't for her, people here wouldn't treat you like an outcast," Viola said.

"I'm used to it," Glorine scoffed. "I was an outcast in my own family—and they were white trash! Can't be more of an outcast than that."

Viola remained indignant. "She thinks she's descended from the queen of England. Well, the queen of England never had a son that set fire to twelve barns."

"And then helped put them out!" Glorine cracked. "I tell

you—Plain Glen gave new meaning to the words 'volunteer fireman.'"

"She'll change her tune when she finds out about your appointment with the adjutant," Viola huffed. Glorine had been fighting to get Plain Glen's prison term reduced.

Glorine's close-set eyes narrowed into a squint. A green station wagon was pulling into her driveway across the street. "Is that who I think it is?" she said. Her voice was sergeantlike. A gangly, baby-faced man in an Agway jumpsuit scrambled out of the wagon and knocked on Glorine's front door. Viola clasped her throat and licked her lips. She pushed the leopard headband back in place and readjusted her hair in front. She had a crush on that man. No one knew.

He was Dave L. Garson, the artificial inseminator, who performed for dairy farmers and cattle breeders in four counties; he had three children and a wife named Flo. In the off-season, he slunk around Dustin, knocking on doors of women whose husbands weren't home, demonstrating a line of telephone-answering machines. The third message on the demo tape was an obscene phone call, which he followed up with one or two dirty Polaroids of himself. The wives who responded found themselves on a list in his wallet. Guiltily, they filled Flo's cup when she did her annual collection for cerebral palsy. Neither Flo nor Dave got too far with Glorine. "I backed him out of the kitchen with a carving knife," she bragged. "'One false move, Garson,' I said, 'and you'll be walking around with nothing between your legs but a breeze!'"

Viola didn't laugh. She didn't hear. She was praying that Dave would come into the luncheonette next. Her prayers were not answered. "He's going home," she reported. "He'll probably have lunch at home." Her voice was sullen. She sighed heavily and snatched a chocolate bar from the rack.

Glorine eyed the progress of the bar as Viola unwrapped it and brought it to her lips. "You ain't gone and had something to *do* with Dave L. Garson, have you?" she asked.

A haughty expression passed over Viola's face. She bit the bar in half and stored the chunk in her cheek. "Something," she admitted. "But not *everything*."

"When?"

"May 17."

Glorine's eyes flashed. "And you're waiting for him to come back and *finish*?"

"He *said* he would." Viola began to weep.

"There's two things I can't stomach," Glorine lectured. "One is liars. The other is hypocrites. He's both. He and Dustin deserve each other. But he don't deserve you."

"God, it hurts," Viola said between sniffs.

Glorine reached across the counter and patted Viola's swollen, bejeweled hand. "As long as I'm in Dustin," she promised, "anybody who hurts you will pay for it! I ain't half-Irish and half-Injun for nothing!" She slid down off the stool and waited with her hand on the latch of the door while Viola alternately boo-hooed and chewed up the chocolate bar. "You okay?" she asked when Viola had wiped her eyes. "Because I got to go now."

"I'll just eat myself sick. That's all."

"Viola, you got to have backbone to survive," Glorine preached. "That's what got Eleanor in trouble. Lack of backbone." Eleanor had been Viola's best friend before Glorine. A farmer's wife, she was hypoglycemic and had eight children. One day when the family came home for supper, there was nothing on the table. Eleanor was playing the violin. She refused to stop. They had her carted away to the Gardnerville State Mental Hospital.

"You're right," Viola whispered soberly.

"It ain't as good as front-bone." Glorine grinned. "But you can't have everything." Viola smiled. "Good," Glorine said. "I like to leave you with a little smile."

"Don't go."

"I got to." Glorine's features took on a seductive softness.

She lowered her eyes and her voice became velvety. "I promised the road crew a surprise this afternoon. I got to work on it."

"What is it?" Viola asked jealously.

"I'm going as a platinum blond!"

Viola exhaled a little noise of excitement.

"If I ruled the world," Glorine said, "it would take a year to put a pipe in a road. Them little hard hats really turn me on!" She looked out the screen door at the flashing red lights.

"God, I wish my husband was in jail," Viola sighed. The women were silent a moment. "You're damned if you do, and you're damned if you don't," Viola summarized, glancing out her porthole onto Highway 6. The town clerk and the woman who ran the Gift & Tackle Shoppe were advancing conspiratorially toward the luncheonette in huge, crisp housedresses. "Oh, no, here come the Three Fates," Viola said.

"Let them make their own coffee," Glorine said. Viola looked shocked. "I mean it," Glorine insisted. "Come on over and keep me company while you're still in a good mood."

"How?" Viola asked.

Glorine punched the light switch and flipped the Marlboro sign in the screen door to "Closed." "That's how," she said. She took Viola by the hand and pulled her out onto the crossroads. Viola slunk across the baking pavement, keeping in Glorine's shadow to the extent she could.

Nine-year-old Aura and eight-year-old Mae were sitting at the foot of the stairs when Glorine came in. They'd been into the lipstick and rouge at her dressing table and looked like miniature prostitutes. "Did that man see you like that?" Glorine bellowed, hands on her skimpy hips.

"That man asked for you!" Aura bellowed back. Viola withdrew to the kitchen. She hated arguments. Glorine's house was always filled with arguments.

"Don't you ever open the door to that man. Stay out of my

makeup. And stay out of my room. How many times do I have to tell you that? When I leave you two in charge, I want you to listen to what I say!"

"Yes, ma'am! We'll stay out of your room! We won't never lock Glen Junior in your closet again!" Aura's voice rang with challenge. Glen Junior was the four-year-old terror no one would babysit for twice. The closet punishment was saved for his most extreme behavior.

Glorine braced herself. "What'd he do now?"

"Took the hammer to your TV," Aura reported gleefully. "Now you only get channel 11."

"Took the hammer to my TV," Glorine said in a soft, peeved mimic of Aura's voice. She cursed and stalked up the stairs. Aura winced and Mae put her fingers in her ears. Glorine threw open the closet door so hard it banged against the wall and knocked a bottle of toilet water off her dressing table. Glen Junior sat fearlessly among her shoes, sucking on the heel of one of Glorine's dyed-to-match red spikes. His mouth was a round red O.

"Put my goddamn shoe down before you ruin it!" she screamed, wrestling the heel from his mouth and hurling it across the room. She raised her hand to beat him. He gazed at her steadily, waiting. Her voice had the power and whine of a chain saw. "You ruin my shoes!" she roared. "You ruin my TV. You break everything you touch. You throw rocks at cars. Nobody in this town can stand you and I'm stuck with you. I ought to shut this door and lock it forever!"

A satisfied look settled onto Glen Junior's face. Glorine lowered her hand. "Get out," she whispered. When he wouldn't move out of the shoes, she sank down at the foot of her unmade bed.

Glorine had intended to be a country western singer. In West Virginia, they said she was as good as Tanya Tucker. It was Glen Junior she blamed. If he hadn't been conceived on the train to New York, she would have gone agent hunting instead of husband hunting. She wanted to beat the living day-lights out of him for ruining her life, but Plain Glen had made that *his* job. Only since the arrest had Glorine's brown-eyed mistake been free of bruises.

She reached down and picked up her red high heel. It matched her red lace formal, the one she had intended to wear to auditions. She gave it back to Glen Junior. "Here," she said. "Suck on it. It ain't doing me no good."

It was ninety-three degrees by one o'clock. Viola sat at Glorine's aqua dinette set, fanning her throat and uttering small self-indulgent sighs. Her right hand strayed regularly across the table to a package of candy corn. She had one eye on the television set in the living room where the year-old twins, Ed and Earl, were watching an old John Wayne–Maureen O'Hara movie from separate playpens. She expected the kitchen phone to ring at any moment with Bud's quiet, cold reprimand: "Get back where you belong!"

Glorine was perched on a stool at the counter with Red Cross cotton taped all around her hairline, applying platinum hair coloring. She had a pink pearl hand mirror propped up between a Kleenex box and her salt and pepper shakers so she could see what she was doing. The chemicals filled the kitchen with a professional stink, masking the sour odor of soiled diapers and dirty dishes. Aura and Mae had tied Glen Junior to the fence with their jump ropes for the duration of the hair coloring. All three were visible through the screen door, standing in the shade. They were watching the new neighbor lady, who had dressed herself in a straw hat and a bathing suit to paint her lawn furniture white.

"I tried to tell her what she was doing was a waste of time," Glorine said. "'Everybody here sits inside,' I said. She said, 'Is that so?' But she kept right on painting that lawn furniture. Where she comes from, they all sit outside."

"Where's that—heaven?" Viola said. She resented the lack

of privacy in Dustin. Properties had developed haphazardly between the crossroads and the Lackawanna Railroad tracks. Back yards faced front yards. Side yards became semipublic. It brought out the worst in people.

Glorine studied the hair-coloring package. "I have to rinse this crap off in forty-five minutes."

Aura burst through the screen door, letting it slam in her sister's face. She blinked at the sticky gray cream lathered all over her mother's head. "That man is out there!"

"*What* man?" Glorine asked.

"That man with the green car."

Glorine and Viola hooked eyes. "It can't be!" Viola gasped. She and Glorine rushed to the screen door. Dave L. Garson's green station wagon was parked in the new lady's gravel driveway. He was leaning against it with his baseball cap pulled down over his eyes, smiling and insidious, asking the new lady questions. She had taken off her straw hat to answer.

"It can't be, but it is," Glorine said.

"Look how red her legs are!" Viola cried. Her voice was hysterical. "She's going to peel!"

"Shhhh!" Glorine warned. They watched the new lady put down her paintbrush and dab her arms and fingers daintily with Glorine's turpentine.

"Don't go in, Dave," Viola coached in a whisper.

The new lady self-consciously tucked her bottom further into her bathing suit. She went up her back steps sideways and held the door open for the artificial inseminator.

"I'm going to kill myself!" Viola sobbed. Dave looked suspiciously over his shoulder at Glorine's back yard.

"Get down!" Glorine hissed, jumping away from the door. Viola dropped to all fours. Her big tears fell on the floor. Aura and Mae stifled giggles when they saw her huge red behind shaking like Jell-O.

"How am I going to stop him?" Glorine muttered. "*Think*, Viola."

"He goes to *your* house, *her* house, everywhere but *my* house!" Viola wept.

"Get up, Vi!"

"No! I'm right where I belong—on the floor!"

"Don't you go getting in no slump on me, Viola Planjek," Glorine said. "Not when I need you the most. We got to stop him!"

"He's not a bad person, Glorine."

Glorine stared at Viola in disbelief. "And I thought *I* was a fool," she said. Impatiently, she picked up the telephone and dialed four numbers.

"Who are you calling?"

"Marshal Jim."

"No!"

"Yes!"

A rapid busy signal echoed loudly in Glorine's ear. She slammed down the phone. "Damn it all!" she said. "He's got the phone off the hook again! Wouldn't you know it—Dustin has the only marshal in the country who can't miss an episode of 'One Life to Live.'"

She turned her attention to her daughters. "Girls, mind your brother," she said. Her face brightened suddenly. "Better yet, bring him here. Hurry!" She waited with her eyes on the screen door until Mae's face reappeared. Mae rolled her forehead back and forth against the mesh.

"Aura says to tell you don't be mad," Mae said.

"He's gone?" Glorine asked. Mae nodded. Glorine pounded the dinette with fury. "Why?" she beseeched the ceiling. "Why can't I get no help around here?"

She looked around the counter for her cigarettes, found them, and lit one. "You and your sister keep Viola company," she said wearily to Mae.

Her Glen-finding routine always began at the crossroads. She made sure he wasn't dead, then she searched the front and back yards of all thirteen houses one by one. She was half-done this time when she passed the marshal's house and heard the TV blaring. His front yard was bare dirt dragged clean by Wallace, a watchdog who had been chained to a stake in front for twelve years. "You seen Glen?" Glorine asked Wallace. Wallace hit his bony tail on the ground twice.

Bees were buzzing in the hollyhocks Bertha Shotz had planted to screen out the marshal's ugly yard. Flowers from her garden won prizes year after year at the county fair. Glorine parted the hollyhocks. Glen Junior was standing belligerently in the middle of Bertha's double Gloriosa daisies, facing the other direction. "You!" she bellowed. He jumped and turned around. "Get over here!"

He trampled the daisies obediently. Glorine grabbed his T-shirt neckline. "You want to make your mother real happy for once in her miserable life?" she demanded with clenched teeth. "If you do, then you just go over next door to us where you saw that new lady painting that furniture and you do whatever you want to that big green car!"

Glen Junior's face became galvanized with purpose. Swinging his shoulders in the direction of the enemy, he trudged off and disappeared behind the hedge that separated Glorine's house from the post office. As she crossed the street, Glorine could already hear the sound of glass shattering and metal crunching. Glen Junior was emptying his secret storehouse of large sharp rocks on Dave L. Garson's wagon.

"The night my sister loved me—but what kind of love?" Glorine was pretending to read the title story of her romance magazine when Dave L. Garson slammed through the back door. He lunged around the kitchen, awkward as a Great Dane on ice. His nose was bleeding slowly. Pain and insult were blended in his infantile eyes. "Where is that brat?" he snorted.

"Which one?" Glorine asked.

"Where *is* he? I'm going to blister his butt! Did you see what he did to my car?"

"I been all over the neighborhood myself, looking for him," Glorine said.

"Look what he did!" He pointed indignantly to his bleeding nose. "I'm putting that kid in jail next to his father!"

"*His* father ain't in jail," Glorine said proudly. "*His* father is a singer."

Dave was momentarily confused. "You know what I mean," he said. He stomped his foot and gathered his big hands into boyish fists. "I want that kid!" With wild eyes, he searched the kitchen for hiding places. He marched over to the pantry and threw open the door. Viola was cringing inside on all fours. "What in the hell are *you* doing here?" he asked.

Inexplicably, she bleated, "Moooo."

Dave turned to Glorine, bewildered. She put a wet dish towel to his face. "Sit down and I'll clean you up like a good neighbor," she said.

He grabbed the towel out of her hands. "I'll do it myself."

"Not *that* side," she said as he dabbed his nose. He looked at the towel suspiciously.

"Christ! Peanut butter!" He threw the towel on the floor and strode toward the front door. "You're going to be sorry, Glorine," he said, slamming it. "I'm getting the marshal." Striking out across her front yard, he called over his shoulder, "You're getting sued!"

"Not till 'General Hospital' is over!" Glorine called back.

Standing in front of the medicine cabinet mirror, Glorine happily removed her hot pink rollers and tossed them into the Chandler's shoe box in Glen Junior's lap. He was seated on the sink in the position of honor. Glorine had carried the twins upstairs for the occasion, handing Ed to Aura and Earl to Mae. All five were chewing Tootsie Rolls, Glorine's gift when she was pleased. Their mouths were going peaceably, but their faces were vaguely horrified. Something had gone wrong with the hair coloring. Glorine's hair was bright orange.

"Wasn't that a stitch?" she hooted. "Seeing Dave L. Garson get a rock in the nose!" The children snickered and gloated. "We ain't had fun like that in a long time, have we, kids?" Glorine teased and combed her hair into a smooth bouffant. "Too bad old Viola couldn't enjoy it," she murmured. Viola had stayed in the pantry binging on marshmallows and grape jam. When Bud called, she was glassy-eyed from the sugar. Glorine had fixed her two cups of instant coffee and walked her back to the luncheonette.

"Hold your noses," Glorine warned, spraying a layer of perfumy lacquer over the finished hairdo. Aura and Mae pinched the twins' nostrils shut. The twins opened their mouths to breathe and their candy fell on the floor.

"Leave it," Glorine said. "There's more in my purse." She brushed the extra hairs off her shoulders and leisurely descended the stairs. All five children followed her to the front door and stood there with their faces pressed into the screen, mesmerized by the sight of their mother, her head on fire in the afternoon sun, walking down Route 1 in her red spikes, late for her visit with the road crew. The temperature had climbed to ninety-eight degrees, and she knew there wasn't a man among them who hadn't been checking his watch, waiting for the surprise.

Other Iowa Short Fiction Award Winners

1986
Eminent Domain, Dan O'Brien
Judge: Iowa Writers' Workshop

1986
Resurrectionists, Russell Working
Judge: Tobias Wolff

1985
Dancing in the Movies,
Robert Boswell
Judge: Tim O'Brien

1984
Old Wives' Tales,
Susan M. Dodd
Judge: Frederick Busch

1983
Heart Failure, Ivy Goodman
Judge: Alice Adams

1982
Shiny Objects, Dianne Benedict
Judge: Raymond Carver

1981
The Phototropic Woman,
Annabel Thomas
Judge: Doris Grumbach

1980
Impossible Appetites,
James Fetler
Judge: Francine du Plessix Gray

1979
Fly Away Home, Mary Hedin
Judge: John Gardner

1978
A Nest of Hooks, Lon Otto
Judge: Stanley Elkin

1977
The Women in the Mirror,
Pat Carr
Judge: Leonard Michaels

1976
The Black Velvet Girl,
C. E. Poverman
Judge: Donald Barthelme

1975
*Harry Belten and the
Mendelssohn Violin Concerto*,
Barry Targan
Judge: George P. Garrett

1974
*After the First Death There Is
No Other*, Natalie L. M. Petesch
Judge: William H. Gass

1973
The Itinerary of Beggars,
H. E. Francis
Judge: John Hawkes

1972
The Burning and Other Stories,
Jack Cady
Judge: Joyce Carol Oates

1971
*Old Morals, Small Continents,
Darker Times*,
Philip F. O'Connor
Judge: George P. Elliott

1970
The Beach Umbrella,
Cyrus Colter
Judges: Vance Bourjaily
and Kurt Vonnegut, Jr.